Felix Frost
Time Detective
GHOST PLANE

Eleanor Hawken is also the author of

Felix Frost Time Detective: Roman Riddle

Sammy Feral's Diaries of Weird

Sammy Feral's Diaries of Weird: Yeti Rescue

Sammy Feral's Diaries of Weird: Hell Hound Curse

Sammy Feral's Diaries of Weird: Dragon Gold

Sammy Feral's Diaries of Weird: Vampire Attack

The Blue Lady

The Grey Girl

Felix Frost
Time Detective
GHOST PLANE

Eleanor Hawken

Quercus

To Luke and Dylan – you rock my world!

First published in Great Britain in 2016 by
Quercus Editions Ltd
Carmelite House
50 Victoria Embankment
London EC4Y 0DZ

An Hachette UK company

Text © 2016 Eleanor Hawken
Illustrations © 2016 Steve May

A CIP catalogue record for this book is available from the British Library

PB 978 1 84866 562 0
EBOOK 978 1 84866 816 4

10 9 8 7 6 5 4 3 2 1

Typeset by Tim Rose

Printed and bound in Great Britain by Clays Ltd, St Ives plc

1
Living History

'Just think of all the things we could do our history project on, Felix.' Missy beamed as she and Felix walked out of the school gates. 'We could fire up the time machine and go anywhere!'

Most school projects are as dull as a dust cloud in a far corner of the galaxy, Felix thought to himself. *But a 'living history' project, well, that's different — it holds all kinds of exciting possibilities, especially when you own a time machine . . .*

Felix shook his mop of scruffy brown hair and frowned.

No. Time machines are dangerous . . . dangerous . . . dangerous!

'We can't use the time machine, Missy, you know that.' Felix sighed. 'It's too risky. Don't you remember what happened last time? We were nearly smashed to a pulp in Emperor Nero's arena! Not to mention the fact that we probably upset the space-time continuum. And I had to eat stuffed rat!'

Missy rolled her eyes. 'Relax, Felix.'

It was only a few weeks ago that Felix and Missy had used Felix's homemade time machine to travel back to Ancient Rome and solve the mystery of a Roman skeleton. The adventure had not been completely smooth sailing. In fact, they had been lucky to escape with their lives.

'What harm could a little bit of innocent time travelling possibly do?' Missy shrugged and batted her eyelashes. 'I say we fire up the time machine this evening!'

Comet tails and asteroids! Felix thought, letting out an exasperated sigh. *Does Missy have to argue with everything I say? I'm a genius — doesn't that mean anything?* Felix looked at Missy's resolute expression. *No, apparently my genius means nothing at all to her . . .*

Missy was the first person outside Felix's family who had ever discovered just how clever he really was.

Felix Frost = child genius.

His exceptional intellect was something Felix had fought long and hard to keep top secret. He had always wondered how someone would react if they knew the truth about him. *Maybe they'd offer me a Nobel Prize right then and there on the spot?* he had wondered. *Or make motivational T-shirts and posters with things I've said on them. Would they make me a knight of the realm? Build a statue in my honour? Name a science lab after me? Or would I just be locked up, and probed and prodded by scientists until there was nothing but stewed cabbage inside my skull . . . ?*

But Missy Six didn't treat Felix any differently from anybody else. Nothing had changed since she'd discovered he was much cleverer than he let on. She still liked to argue with everything Felix said and did.

Felix and Missy made their way through the crowd of chattering school children and into the freedom of the outside world. The school bell was still distantly ringing behind them as they scuffed their shoes along the pavement, both deep in thought.

Just my luck that I get paired up to write a history project with the one person who knows I invented a time machine. Felix nearly tripped on his untied shoelaces as he tried to keep up with Missy. *Of course she'll want to use the time machine to do some research. She'll never take no for an answer . . .*

'I won't take no for an answer, Felix. We have a week to write the history project and we have to work together,' Missy reminded him, charging ahead. 'I've had a few ideas about what we could base our project on.' Her blonde corkscrew hair bounced around her as she excitedly marched down the street. 'We could . . .

- ❋ *Unravel the secret of Stonehenge*
- ❋ *Solve the riddle of the Sphinx*
- ❋ *Learn the truth about South America's famous Crystal Skull*
- ❋ *Discover the identity of Jack the Ripper*
- ❋ *Meet King Arthur . . .'*

'Hold it right there, Missy.' Felix stopped walking and held his hands out to halt her. 'We have to write a "living history" project for school. That means that whatever we write about needs to have happened within *living* memory. The memory of people still *alive*. The things you're talking about happened

5

hundreds of years ago – there's no one still alive to remember King Arthur.'

'Merlin could still be alive for all we know.' She shrugged. 'He's a wizard – who knows how long they live?' Felix frowned and rolled his eyes at Missy's attempt to argue with him. She folded her arms in front of her chest and scowled. 'Got any better ideas then, genius?'

'Shush!' Felix quickly looked around, checking that no one had heard. 'Not so loud with the "genius" stuff. It's meant to be a secret, remember?'

'Calm down, no one heard,' Missy said, glancing around to check no one was listening in.

'And actually, yes,' Felix said quietly, 'I do have a few better ideas for our project. We could . . .

⁎ *Build a basic computer with no Internet access and re-enact the eighties*

⁎ *Write about the discovery of DNA (I've been meaning to retest my genetic code for a while)*

⁎ *Research the technology glitches that occurred when the clocks struck midnight in the year 2000.'*

Missy rolled her eyes. 'Your ideas are boring, Felix. Mine are much more interesting.'

'But your ideas involve time travel, Missy,' Felix pointed out again. 'And time travel is dangerous, stupid and . . .'

'Fine!' Missy snapped. 'What if I told you I had a really cool idea for our project that didn't involve time travel?'

'I'm listening . . .'

'My great-grandad was a pilot in World War Two. We could write our project about him.'

Felix smiled. 'Now that *is* a cool idea! There were so many incredible scientific leaps in World War Two. The science of weaponry, communications, medicine, industry . . . We could write our project on any one of those things.'

'It's a history project,' Missy reminded him. She shot out her arm to hail a double-decker bus that was driving towards them, before adding, 'Not a science project.'

'Tomorrow's Saturday,' Felix pointed out, ignoring her. 'We could go and visit your great-grandad then, maybe? We could interview him and record what he says. I can't afford to buy a video camera, but I could make one out of a basic lens, some copper wiring, a motherboard and some—'

'We can use our phones to record him, numbskull.' Missy thumbed around in her bag until she found her bus pass.

Numbskull! Who's she calling numbskull? Since when does being able to build a video camera from household objects make someone a numbskull?!

'No need for one of your fancy electronic sessions. And you are going to LOVE what Gaga Bill has to tell you tomorrow. The story of the ghost plane will blow your mind . . .'

Without another word Missy leaped on to the bus and waved goodbye to Felix.

Blow my mind? Felix shook his head, watching the bus drive away from him and out of sight. *I doubt that very much. My mind's created a homemade rocket launcher, X-ray glasses AND a time machine. There's not a lot that could blow it . . .*

It was only a short walk from the bus stop to Felix's family home. The front door was already ajar as Felix walked up to it. He pushed it open, expecting to smell his mum's horrible cooking wafting through the hallway from the kitchen. But there was nothing. He could hear the hum of the TV coming from the living room.

Freddie and Frank, his older brothers, charged down the stairs, nearly knocking into Felix as the front door swung shut behind him.

'Mum!' screamed Freddie, Felix's oldest brother. 'I can't find my football shorts!'

'They're in your bottom drawer, darling,' Felix's mum called back from the kitchen.

'Not those ones, Mum,' Freddie shouted, standing on the bottom stair in just his tight white pants. 'Those have a rip in them from when I skid-kicked the winning goal into the net last game, remember?'

Felix's mum appeared from the kitchen; she was carrying her handbag in one hand and two sports drinks for Freddie and Frank in the other. 'Well, your other shorts are still in the wash. Can't you borrow some of Frank's?'

'No he can't!' grunted Frank.

Felix heard the noise of the TV suddenly turn off

in the living room and his father appeared in the hallway. 'Time to watch my boys in action yet?' he asked.

'Slight crisis,' Mum said with a frown. 'Freddie's football shorts are—'

'I can mend your shorts,' Felix said to Freddie, shrugging off his school bag and kicking off his shoes.

'So now you can sew as well as do degree-level physics?' Freddie said with a smirk.

'No,' Felix said simply. 'I've created a laser that can fuse any two things together. I'm pretty sure it will work on cotton particles and—'

Frank chuckled, looking in the hallway mirror and inspecting his gelled hair. 'Felix probably doesn't even know what football shorts are, Freddie.'

Felix defended himself. 'Of course I know what football shorts are. And I know about shin pads, and football boots and goal nets. I've told you before – I *like* football. What's not to like? The mechanics of ball flight . . . the biomechanics of a human leg kicking a ball . . . the mathematics of ball-flight curvature . . . the topspin needed to—'

'Stop trying to ruin football for us, Felix,' grunted Freddie.

'That's enough,' Mum snapped. 'Felix, if you really can use that clever little head of yours to fix your brother's shorts then please can you do it quickly?' She reached across and ruffled Felix's hair with a fond smile. 'Oh, you'll have to make yourself dinner this evening,' she added, grabbing her coat from a hook on the wall. 'Your dad and I are going to watch Frank and Freddie play football and then we're taking them for pizza afterwards.'

'I like pizza too,' Felix reminded her.

'Well, there might be a frozen one in the freezer,' his mum said absently, pulling on her coat.

'If not you could always make one with a laser,' Frank joked.

'And after you've eaten you've got chores to do,' Mum said. 'Remember?'

'Like you'd ever let me forget,' Felix muttered so Mum couldn't hear.

'Hurry up then, Felix,' his dad said, picking up Frank and Freddie's boot bags and swinging his car keys around his finger. 'If we don't leave in the next five minutes then the boys will be late for warm-up.'

Felix elbowed past his older brothers and ran up the stairs.

He pushed open the door to his bedroom and flicked on the light.

A small chameleon leaped out from between two

heavy engineering textbooks on a nearby shelf and landed on Felix's shoulder.

'Hi, Einstein.' Felix smiled down at his pet lizard. 'Good day?' Einstein's scales flashed purple for 'Yes', before quickly turning **orange** . . .

Felix had trained his pet chameleon to communicate with him through the changing colours of his scales.

Green = disgust

Red = danger

Yellow = happy

Blue = sad

Orange = worry

Purple = yes

Pink = no

'Don't worry, buddy,' Felix reassured him. 'Mum's not cooking dinner this evening. I'll make us something that's actually edible. But first . . .'

Felix rummaged around in the large wooden chest that sat next to his bed. He picked up various inventions and tossed them over his shoulder as he tried to find what he was looking for. 'My pocket lie detector, my nano radio, homemade fart gas, rocket launcher, X-ray glasses . . . Ah-ha! There it is, my particle-fusing laser.'

Felix's bedroom door swung open behind him and Freddie walked in without being invited. He shook his old pair of sweaty football shorts at Felix and then looked around the room.

The walls of Felix's room were covered in scientific equations that Felix had thought up over the years. The shelves were stuffed with science books only top professors could understand and piled high around the room were old circuit boards, test tubes, atomic models and tools that belonged to Felix.

'Are you sure we're related?' Freddie muttered.

'Yes,' Felix said, flicking the on switch to his particle-fusing laser and directing it at Freddie's torn football shorts. 'I did DNA testing on all of us years ago.'

Freddie looked at his younger brother with a confused expression as Felix moved the laser along the tear in the shorts and the material fused back together, mending them as good as new. After a few seconds Felix switched off the laser and tossed the shorts back at Freddie.

As Freddie turned to leave, something caught his eye.

'Why do you have Mum's old microwave in here?' he asked, pointing at the ancient appliance that Felix had rewired into a time machine.

Felix felt his face go bright red.

Haloes and galaxies! Of all the things in my bedroom Freddie could notice . . .

'Umm,' Felix said. 'I thought I could fix it, but . . .'

'Mum's cooking has blasted it beyond repair?' Freddie joked.

Felix nodded and looked down at the floor. 'Ah-ha.'

Freddie scrunched up his face. 'I don't believe there's any machine in this world that you couldn't pick apart and rebuild.'

For a split second, Felix nearly opened his mouth and spilled everything . . . *I didn't repair it because I've used it to build a time machine. A time machine that took me and my best friend back to Ancient Rome. We nearly died there. Now she wants to time travel again and I don't. It's too dangerous. What if we die or get stuck there? What if we change the course of history? Maybe I should destroy the time machine? What if I don't and it gets into the wrong hands? What do you think I should do?*

The words danced on Felix's lips, and for a moment he wished he could speak to his older brother about the problems he faced.

Freddie would never understand, he realized. *He'd think I was crazy and have me shipped off to a loony bin, or even worse — he'd tell Mum.*

Freddie held up his mended football shorts.

'Thanks,' he muttered under his breath, as Felix continued to stare at him.

'Just you and me tonight, buddy,' Felix said to Einstein, as Freddie left the room. The small lizard crawled down his arm and rested on his hand. 'I might not be able to speak to my brothers about my problems but I can always speak to you. I need to fill you in on what happened at school today. Missy and I have to write a history project together. She wants to use the time machine . . .'

2
Gaga Bill

Felix and Missy arranged to meet on Saturday morning outside her great-grandad Bill's house.

'Did you bring Einstein with you?' Missy asked as Felix approached the small semi-detached house at the other end of town. She was sitting on the garden wall waiting for him.

Flying Fibonacci! What's wrong with, 'Hello Felix, how are you?' No, she'd rather hear about my pet lizard . . .

'No,' he answered. 'Carrying a lizard everywhere you go tends to attract the wrong kinds of questions.'

Missy leaped down from the wall. 'But you'll bring him with us when we go time travelling, won't you?'

'We're not going time travelling again, Missy,' Felix said, frowning. 'We can do our project on World War Two using the facts your great-grandad gives us.'

Missy gave Felix a knowing smile. 'Hmm, you won't feel like that once you've heard the story about the ghost plane.'

'Oh yeah.' Felix smirked. 'I'm sure my mind will be well and truly blown . . .' he joked.

'It will be,' she said seriously.

Missy led the way up the garden path, then reached up and rang the doorbell. After what felt like ages, the door slowly creaked open and a very elderly, frail man poked his head out. He was wearing a smart shirt and tie and the grey hair he had left was neatly swept over to one side.

'Missy!' The old man beamed, his milky eyes lighting up when he saw the young girl with corkscrew blonde hair on his doorstep. 'What a lovely surprise.'

'I called you last night, Gaga Bill, remember?' Missy reminded him. 'I told you that we were going to come round and see you today.'

'That's right.' He smiled and nodded. 'Your school project. I remember now. You'll have to forgive me,' he apologized to Felix. 'Brain cells aren't what they used to be when you get to my ripe old age.'

He sounds American, Felix thought. *Missy's never mentioned that her family came from America.*

Missy reached up and threw her arms around the old man, hugging him carefully. 'Good to see you, Gaga Bill. Can we come in?'

'Of course.' The old man smiled, waving Missy and Felix through the front door and closing it behind them.

Missy introduced them. 'This is Felix. And this is Chief Master Sergeant Bill Hudson, but I call him Gaga Bill. And this . . .' A small white Scottie dog padded out of the living room and enthusiastically sniffed Missy's scuffed shoes, his tail wagging madly. 'This is Frosty.'

'Hello, Frosty.' Felix bent down and petted the small dog, letting it lick his hands in greeting. 'And hello, sir,' he said to Bill. 'Nice to meet you.'

'Please, just call me Bill.' The old man waved his hands dismissively. 'Can I get you both something to drink? I've got some mango juice in the fridge.'

Missy nodded. 'Yum, yes please.'

'You two go and sit down, I'll bring the juice through.' Bill hobbled towards the kitchen and Frosty followed closely at his heels.

Missy led Felix into the living room and towards a battered old sofa. Before sitting down, Felix wandered around the room, gazing at what he saw. A large grandfather clock ticked away in a corner, and the walls were lined with dozens of old black-and-white photographs.

Wow, Bill's whole life is up on these walls . . .

There were rows of pictures of Bill throughout the years. There was one black-and-white picture in which Bill looked about as old as Felix. In it he stood in front of a small aeroplane with another boy the same age, both of them grinning from ear to ear. There were pictures of Bill when he was slightly older in his US Air Force uniform, pictures of him posing proudly with medals on his chest, and pictures of him standing next to aeroplanes. As Felix's eyes moved around the room he noticed that the man in the pictures grew older as the pictures changed from black and white to colour. In every picture in which Bill was wearing his uniform, the medals on his chest grew in number as he grew in age.

Bill's military career must have made him as proud as Pythagoras . . .

Among the photographs of people were framed pictures of aeroplanes. Like everything else in the world, Felix had a good working knowledge of aeroplanes. He recognized most of them. *Bombers, fighter planes, passenger jets* – every aircraft you could think of was up on the walls of Bill's living room. There were dozens in total. **They look like framed postcards,** Felix thought absently.

On the side table beside Felix was a framed picture of Bill when he was a young man, standing with a pretty woman.

'That's Gaga Bill on his wedding day to my great-grandma Stella.' Missy pointed to the photo. 'Stella died before I was born.'

Poor Bill, Felix thought to himself. **He's been on his own for years . . .**

'Gaga Bill was born in America,' Missy said. 'He trained with the US Air Force and was based just outside London during World War Two.'

'That's how I met my wife . . .' said Bill, coming into the room carrying a tray with shaky hands. He put the tray with glasses of juice and a plate of biscuits down on the coffee table. 'Please, help yourselves . . .' Bill said.

Felix didn't need to be told twice. He dived forward and picked up a biscuit, hungrily chomping away on it before washing it down with a large gulp of mango juice. 'What planes did you fly?' he asked, swallowing another mouthful of juice.

'Light bomber aircraft were my home for years.'
Bill gave Felix a guarded smile. 'Apache dive
bombers, Warhawks, Hellcats . . .'

*Wow, planes had some pretty cool names back
in the day . . .*

'You must have seen some gnarly action from the
cockpits of bomber planes during the war,' Felix
said.

'You don't want to hear about any of that stuff,'
Bill replied, looking down at his impeccably
polished shoes.

'Are you kidding me?' Felix blurted out. 'Of
course I . . . ouch!'

Missy elbowed him hard in the ribs and
whispered under her breath, 'Gaga Bill doesn't like
to talk about some of the things he saw in the war.'

Bill slowly sat himself down on a faded armchair
and Frosty sat obediently at his feet.

'I hope and pray that you kids never have to see
any of the sights I had to see back in those days.
War is evil. The less said about it the better.'

Felix gave Missy a confused look. *Isn't that why
we're here? To ask about the war?*

'Wait . . .' Missy whispered to Felix, as if reading his mind.

'Flying planes was my life,' Bill recounted fondly. 'Until I met Stella and that all changed. Marrying Stella was the happiest day of my life.' Bill looked over at the old picture of his wedding day. 'After the war ended I stayed here in England. Our son was born, and years later I became a grandfather when Debbie was born. And then I became a great-grandfather when Missy here came along.' He smiled at his great-granddaughter fondly. 'When you live to as old an age as I am, Felix, you see an awful lot . . . have so many stories to tell.'

'I was hoping you'd tell us the mystery of the ghost plane, Gaga,' Missy said, reaching into her pocket and pulling out her mobile phone. 'And we'll record what you say. I thought we could use the story for our history project.'

'Missy and I are doing a school project on "living history",' Felix explained. 'We have to write about something that happened within living memory.'

'How wonderful!' Bill shuffled forward in his armchair, getting himself comfortable. 'I'd love to help you with your project. And as I said before, the Blitz, bombings, death, destruction – these aren't things a fella wants to talk too much about. And they aren't things for the ears of kids, that's for sure. But the mystery of the ghost plane, now that's something I'm always happy to tell.'

Missy set her phone to record and held it up so she could video Bill. 'Why don't you start by telling us about coming to live in England during the war, and about your war training.'

'Pfff.' Bill shook his head. 'Flying missions and air raids – all I can tell you about those is that I hope you never see such things in your lifetime. Every day when I went up in the skies I never knew if I'd be coming down again. You never knew if each day was your last. Every breakfast, every sunset – would it be the last you ever saw? No, the less I say about that the better. And the story of the ghost plane is far more interesting than aircraft training. It's a story that will set your imaginations alight and have you lying awake at night . . .'

Felix sat forward, intrigued. 'Go on . . .'

'A story that never had an ending . . . one of my life's greatest unsolved mysteries . . .'

Felix felt the hairs on his arms stand to attention. *An unsolved mystery . . . this is right up my street . . .*

Bill sat back in his chair and gazed off into the distance as he remembered. 'The ghost plane. The one story that has haunted me all these long years . . .'

3
The Ghost Plane

'As a boy I'd always dreamed of being a pilot. Of soaring through the skies like a bird. I dreamed that I'd fly my plane up over the fields and farms where I grew up back in Virginia – in America – the people below waving up at me like I was some kind of superhero. My best friend, Archie, he and I were inseparable – always wanted the same things in life. Baseball cards, ice-cream flavours – we were so alike people mistook us for brothers. Archie was just like me – dreamed of flying. So when I learned how to fly a small aircraft when I was not much older than you are now, Felix, Archie did too.' Bill paused, his expression distant. 'In 1939 war broke out in Europe – we all saw what was going on and wondered what we could do to help. But in 1941, when America was attacked, well. Archie and I both knew it was our duty to use our knowledge of the skies to fight for our country – fight against evil. We enrolled in the US Air Force, and they trained Archie and me how to fly small bomber planes. In 1942 he and I were sent over here to England – to an RAF base called Daws Hill, just outside London.

'Most American pilots came to England to help the RAF, but we were something different. An all-American team operating on English soil. The Eighth Bomber Command – that's what they used to call us. We called ourselves the "First Eight". We were a special unit of the US military, trained to take to the skies and rain down one helluva heavy bombardment on the enemy below. Our unit had it all – intelligence services, mission-planning staff, air-traffic controllers and us – the pilots.

While it was other men and women's jobs to gather intelligence about the enemy, and plan the best ways to strike at their heart, it was our job to take to the skies and never question command; to always do as we were instructed to do. Every mission, every time we sat in the cockpit of our aircraft, we never knew if we'd be coming back down again. Never knew if each mission would be our last – but we flew without question. Back home in Virginia, and during the war, in the First Eight, I was one of the best pilots around . . . I flew with honour, pride and bravery.'

Galloping Galileo! Felix thought. *Could I ever be that brave? Could I ever fly a plane over enemy territory, knowing that every mission could be my last . . . ?*

'It was 1943,' Bill continued. 'Me, Archie and the rest of the First Eight had been in England for just over a year when this story really begins . . .'

Missy looked up over the top of her mobile phone that she was using to record Bill. 'Had you met Great-Grandma Stella by then?'

'It was the night I met her,' Bill said seriously, 'that this story began . . .

'. . . Archie and I had had a day's training at the airbase. Running over battle tactics, target analysis – nothing out of the ordinary. But that night there was a dance on at the local village hall. You kids might call it a "disco" these days – although I don't know what you do at discos, not the dancing we used to do! Anyway, when Archie and I arrived at the dance she was the first thing I saw. A pretty young girl with blonde ringlets and the sweetest smile. I asked her name; she told me Stella. I asked her to dance; she made me the happiest man alive when she said yes. We danced all night long. Didn't stop for nothing.

Everyone had gone home for the night when we finally drew apart. I promised Stella I'd see her the next day – said I'd take her back to the dance hall again. Archie didn't shut up the whole way back to base – teasing me about falling in love at first sight . . .'

I thought this was a story about a ghost plane? Felix frowned. *Not some puke-inducing love story. Newton's nutcracker!*

'I know what you're thinking.' Bill chuckled at Felix, as though he could read his thoughts. 'What does some soppy love story have to do with a ghost plane? Good question.' He smiled. 'Let me tell you the answer . . .

'I'd been so dizzy in love with Stella that night, I'd completely forgotten that I was scheduled to fly the next day. My orders were to spend the day and night test-flying a new light bomber craft that was being prepared to drop bouncing bombs on the enemy in an up-coming top-secret mission. Now, you remember, I told you before . . .'

'You always obeyed orders . . .' Missy finished off for him. 'No matter what they were.'

'Exactly!' Bill wagged his finger. 'It was our job to do whatever we were told to do. Including test-fly a bouncing bomber mission. But this was different – this was Stella. Nothing was more important than seeing her again. Not my orders, not the top-secret mission, not the trouble I knew

I could get in if I skipped out on doing what I was told to do.'

'So what did you do?' Felix asked.

'Archie had known me since we were boys. One look at my face and he knew I was serious; he knew I'd risk a court martial if it meant seeing Stella again. So Archie did what any best friend would do – he covered for me. He got in my plane and took to the skies. It was Archie who went up on that test mission, so I could stay behind on the ground and see Stella.

'So the next night, I went back to the village dance with Stella – danced all night again – and Archie went up in the plane. Everything else I know about that night I know from accident reports and military files . . .

'That day – the 10th May 1943 – has been burned into my memory forever. Archie's plane took off as planned. He launched it into the skies at fourteen hundred hours, and the engine was in full health – nothing unusual to report. Archie flew that plane up into the horizon, but he didn't return when he was supposed to. The test mission was only meant to take a couple of hours. But as the skies above grew dark the hours came and went, and Archie never reappeared. When morning rolled around word got out around the base that he hadn't come back. But there had been no Mayday call from him, no SOS, no reports of a crash, nothing. It was as if the plane had just vanished.

'Now can you imagine how I felt?' Bill said, sadness etched on his deeply wrinkled face.

No! Felix thought. *How could I ever imagine how it would feel to lose your best friend? Missy's the closest thing I've ever had to a best friend . . . how would I feel if she went missing? Angry . . . sad . . . guilty . . . Who would keep me on my toes if she wasn't around?!*

'I spent that day in a daze – trying for hours to radio Archie, trying to reach him, to find out what had happened. But it got me nowhere. Just when I thought all hope was lost, as the sun was setting on the day and everyone had written Archie off as dead, we saw a shape in the sky. It was a plane coming towards the airbase, coming home. The plane got nearer and we could see it was a light

34

bomber, the very same one that Archie had taken off in the day before. But how could it possibly be the same plane? The fuel would have long before run dry – the tank can't hold more than a couple of hours' worth of fuel. Sure, he could have stopped off and refuelled at another airbase, but if he'd done that he would have radioed to say so. And there was no mistake – it was exactly the same plane flying low towards us. I knew there was something very wrong with that plane – something about the way it cut through the wind didn't look right. Archie was a first-class pilot – the best of the best. But that plane wasn't being flown by the best of the best; it flapped and floundered like there was no one at the wheel at all. And sure enough, as it sank in the sky, speeding down towards the ground at a rate no man could ever survive, I could see . . . in the few split seconds before the plane crash-landed in the airfield I saw into the cockpit – there was no one in there, no one at all.

'The plane burst into flames on impact with the earth. It took nearly four hours to put out the fire. As soon as I could, I climbed up that smouldering, charred wreck of a plane. If Archie's body was in there I knew I had to take him out, take him home to his family in Virginia where he could be buried a hero. But there was nothing – no bones, no trace of Archie to be seen. I guess I'd known as soon as I'd seen the plane crash down to earth without a pilot – Archie wasn't on board when it crashed. No one was. And even stranger – there was no evidence to suggest that a pilot had ejected from the cockpit before the plane crashed. That doomed flight was unpiloted. A ghost plane.'

'Impossible!' Felix muttered.

'Impossible,' Bill echoed in agreement. 'I thought I knew Archie better than I knew myself. But I don't know what became of him after he flew that plane up into the sky. He certainly wasn't on it when it crashed. And I'll never know. No one has ever seen or heard from Archie ever again. He simply vanished into the sky . . . You know, when you live to be as old as I am you have many memories. Some so happy they make your heart burst when you remember, some so sad you can't bring yourself to recollect. But what happened to Archie . . . Well, not knowing has haunted me every day of my life since. I wish I knew.'

Missy's phone beeped in her hands. 'I've run out of memory.' She shook her phone, frustrated. 'I can't record any more.'

'No matter.' Bill smiled, getting to his feet. 'You two ought to be going home now anyway. You kids should be out there running around solving the world's mysteries, not hearing them from an old man like me.' He stretched out his hand to Felix. 'Wonderful to meet you, Felix.'

'It's an honour to have met you, Bill.' Felix shook his hand. 'And thank you for telling us your story. It's amazing – it'll make a great school project.'

'Bye, Gaga Bill.' Missy kissed him on the cheek. 'We'll come again soon.'

'Make sure you do,' Bill said, leading them out into the hallway towards the front door. Both Missy and Felix bent down to say goodbye to Frosty the dog, before saying goodbye to Bill once again and stepping out into the midday sunshine.

'Wow,' Felix said, as Bill closed the door behind them.

Missy smiled. 'I told you he was pretty cool.'

'Liquid nitrogen is pretty cool, Missy. Bill is out-of-this world awesome. I wish I had a great-grandad like that.' Then he turned to her and said seriously, 'If only we could find out what happened to Archie.'

Missy's mouth split into a wide smile. She knew just what Felix meant. 'So you're thinking what I'm thinking . . . ?'

'The time machine?' Felix said slowly. *I'm tempted, but . . .* 'It's too risky.'

'But this is one of the twentieth century's greatest mysteries!' Missy said dramatically, flapping her arms about. 'Who knows what could have happened to Archie! He could have been abducted by aliens, or sucked into a portal to another world, or maybe the plane flew into some kind of Bermuda Triangle and—'

'Whoa, hang on a minute!' Felix stopped her. 'I agree with you – this is one major mystery. But there must be a logical, rational, scientific explanation to it all. Not for one second do I think that aliens or portals had anything to do with it.'

Missy shook her head. 'Well, you can't know that for certain, Felix.'

'Yes I can,' he argued.

'No you can't,' she argued back. 'Not unless we go back and find out what happened to Archie once and for all. Otherwise, we cannot rule out the possibility of aliens.'

'Do I believe aliens exist? Of course I do! To think we're alone in this universe is ridiculous. But do I think aliens had anything to do with Archie's disappearance? No. And if we travelled back in

39

time then I could prove that . . . Ah-ha, I can see what you're trying to do here, Missy . . .'

She smiled. 'Don't tell me you're not just a little bit curious?'

I'm as curious as Schrödinger's cat in a box!

Felix took a deep, deep breath and closed his eyes. 'This has to be the last time . . .'

'Yes!' Missy punched the air.

'OK.' Felix sighed in defeat. 'Let's fire up the time machine and travel back to 1943!'

4
1943

'Felix!' Felix heard his name screamed through the house as soon as he opened the front door. 'Felix!'

'Sounds like Mum's on the warpath . . .' Felix muttered to Missy as they both walked into his small family home.

'Why?' Missy whispered back.

'You haven't done your chores!' Felix's mum appeared in the hallway looking very angry. 'And what time do you call this? Where have you been all morning? You didn't tell us you were going out. Your dad and I were worried.'

'I've been working on my school history project with Missy,' Felix said, taking his jacket off.

'Well, you can't just leave the house and not tell us where you're going,' his mum said sternly.

Sheesh, if Mum worried when I went up the road to Bill's house then she'll freak out more than a nuclear reactor if she knew I was planning to time travel back to World War Two!

'Anyway, Felix –' Mum sounded flustered – 'why are you gallivanting around with your friend when you should be here, at home, doing your chores?'

Felix started to explain. 'Sorry, Mum, but we . . .'

'Save your excuses.' She held up her hand and closed her eyes, as if just the sight of Felix annoyed her. 'You won't get any dinner tonight until you've done everything you need to do.'

No dinner? Thank the galaxies for that! I'd rather eat the fluff between my toes than brave one of Mum's meals when she's in a mood like this!

'What does Felix need to do?' Missy asked. 'Maybe I could help?'

'I don't think so,' Felix's mum said with a slightly patronizing tilt of the head.

'I'm clever too,' Missy said with a frown. 'I mean,

I'm not a genius like Felix is, but I'm way smarter than average.'

Felix's mum turned ghostly grey as the blood drained from her face. She reached for the wall to steady herself and looked as though she was going to burst into floods of tears.

'Missy, Mum didn't know that you know my secret – that I'm a genius,' Felix said, explaining his mum's suddenly strange behaviour.

'Oh, sorry – was I meant to keep it a secret?' Missy said, giving Felix's mum a worried look.

'Felix . . . Felix . . .' Mum stuttered. 'When . . . ?'

'It's a long story, Mum,' Felix said.

One that starts and ends with time travel. 'But we can trust Missy.'

Missy shook her head in agreement.

'Felix,' his mum said with a gulp, 'we've been through this before. It's not just you who'll be cut open and probed by scientists if people know the truth about you. Your father and brothers and I will be sliced up and put under a microscope too!'

'That's a bit dramatic, Mum.'

'Don't speak back to me, Felix!' she snapped, her face turning from grey to red.

Missy reassured her once again. 'I won't say anything, Mrs Frost, I promise.' She held her hand over her heart. 'And, as I was saying before, if I can help Felix with his chores then I will.'

Felix's mum stared at Missy for a long moment. 'He needs to fix the burned-out toaster, rebuild the TV so that we can watch 3D films on it, create 3D glasses so we can watch the new TV, fix the leaking toilet . . .'

'Oh.' Missy nodded.

'It's very sweet of you to offer to help, Missy,' Felix's mum said, still looking her up and down, wondering if she could trust her, 'but I don't think you'll be able to. Felix, you have until eight o'clock to build a 3D TV. The football's on and I've promised your brothers they can watch it in 3D.'

'Can I at least go and say hello to Einstein first?' Felix asked. 'He's been in my room all morning with no one to talk to.'

'He's a lizard,' Mum pointed out. 'He doesn't understand it when you speak to him.'

That's what you think . . .

'Eight o'clock, Felix,' his mum called after him as he and Missy climbed the stairs.

'Einstein!' Felix picked up his pet lizard who was sitting on the end of his unmade bed. 'How you doing, buddy?'

Einstein's scales shone a brilliant **yellow** for happy.

'It's a good thing that you're in a happy mood, Einstein,' Felix said, almost holding his breath. 'Because I have some news for you . . .'

Einstein's scales began to change into a worrying shade of **orange**.

'We're going time travelling again!' Missy announced with a smile.

45

Einstein's scales were now a deep shade of **red**. He knew only too well what time travel meant.

Time travel = DANGER!

'Only we have to wait until Felix does his chores before we go anywhere,' Missy added, disappointed. She looked down at her watch. 'You'd better get cracking if you want to build a 3D TV before the football starts at eight o'clock.'

Felix shrugged. 'I could build a 3D TV with my hands tied behind my back and still have it finished by eight. And my chores can wait. Time travelling first, 3D TV building later.'

Missy frowned. 'But won't your mum spontaneously combust if you don't do your chores?'

'Relax!' Felix reassured her. 'Don't you remember how time travel works? We could go back to 1943 and spend a year there and still be home in time for dinner – not to mention all the chores I have to do. Wherever we go, however long we stay for, we can time travel back to the exact moment we left – remember?'

'I remember,' Missy said, nodding, thinking back to the time they spent two months in Ancient Rome and no time had passed at all when they finally came back home. 'This is so exciting!' She threw her hands into the air dramatically. 'We're going time travelling again! And back to the Second World War – a time of Churchill and Roosevelt and air raids and the jitterbug AND Gaga Bill.'

Felix bent down and began to rummage through the large chest at the side of his bed. Einstein hopped on to his shoulder to watch what he was doing, still glowing a warning shade of red. 'Before we go anywhere we need to pack the right things,' Felix muttered, looking up from the chest and around his room.

What to take . . . what to take . . .

'We could take a penknife,' Missy suggested. 'That could be useful?'

Jumping Jupiter! Felix flashed Missy an unimpressed look. *How is a penknife meant to help with anything? I'll get this done quicker without Missy's suggestions . . .*

Without a word, Felix darted around his room, quickly gathering his most useful tools for the adventure that lay ahead. He took . . .

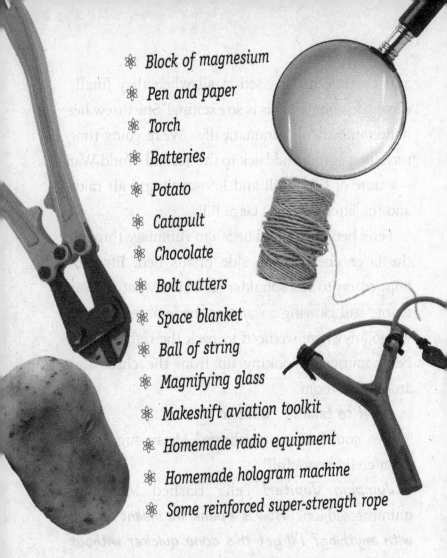

- Block of magnesium
- Pen and paper
- Torch
- Batteries
- Potato
- Catapult
- Chocolate
- Bolt cutters
- Space blanket
- Ball of string
- Magnifying glass
- Makeshift aviation toolkit
- Homemade radio equipment
- Homemade hologram machine
- Some reinforced super-strength rope

Missy watched Felix silently as he tossed each item on to his bed. She began to inspect the things he was throwing down.

'Why are we packing a potato?' she asked.

'To use when the batteries run out, obviously,' Felix muttered, starting to rifle through his large bedside chest once again.

'Does chocolate work as a power source too?' she asked, looking at the large pile of chocolate on the bed.

'Do you have marbles for brains?' Felix said, laughing. 'The chocolate is in case we get hungry. Every good adventurer needs a food supply.'

Missy peered over Felix's shoulder before reaching into the chest and pulling out what looked like a battered old can of deodorant. 'What's this?'

'Camouflage spray,' Felix replied. 'Actually, chuck that on the bed too – it could be useful.'

Felix stood up and surveyed the items on the bed. He nodded to himself and quickly stuffed them into an old rucksack.

'Ready?' Missy said, smiling, once he'd finished packing his bag.

'As I'll ever be,' Felix replied, swinging the heavy bag over his shoulder.

Einstein tried to leap from Felix's shoulder and scramble to safety, but Felix managed to grab him by the tail and shove him in his trouser pocket. 'You're part of the team, Einstein. You're coming too.' Felix didn't need to be able to see Einstein to know that at that moment he'd be glowing radioactive **red**.

'Don't forget this.' Missy tossed Felix the old TV remote control that was an essential part of the time machine.

Felix programmed the time and date – 4pm, 9th May, 1943 into the TV remote – one day before Archie had gone missing – followed by the coordinates for the RAF Daws Hill airbase.

'How did you know those coordinates off by heart?' Missy asked, as they walked towards the middle of the room, preparing to activate the time machine.

'When I was seven years old I had the flu and had to stay off school for a week,' Felix explained. 'I used the free time to memorize the coordinates of every major city, railway station, airport and military base in the world. I always knew it would come in handy . . .'

Standing in the middle of the room, Felix, Missy and Einstein were in the direct line of fire for the time machine's lasers. Felix had built the time machine by accident, when he'd been trying to turn an old microwave oven into a teleporter. He'd angled the lasers inside the machine to shoot out and hit whatever was standing in front of it, blasting enough force and energy to propel that object through time and space.

Felix reached up on to his tiptoes and picked up a small smoky quartz rock that was sitting in the dust.

The small rock was the key to making the time machine work. Felix had discovered that by accident when it had fallen into the path of the lasers and he'd been catapulted back to Ancient Rome.

Felix held the rock in front of his face. 'The final cog in the time machine,' he said with a smile. 'Once I throw the rock into the path of the laser and press the green button on the remote control then we'll soon be whizzing through time and space,' he reminded Missy. 'If you're having second thoughts, then speak up now.'

'No second thoughts here,' Missy said firmly. 'Let's get this time travelling show on the road.'

Here we go again . . .

'Ready.' Felix licked his lips in anticipation. 'One
. . . two . . . three!' He threw the small rock into
the air and pressed the green button on the remote
control.

Suddenly the world began to fade. The crammed bookshelves of Felix's room, the equations he'd scribbled on his bedroom walls – everything began to disappear. The walls and furniture looked as though they were melting away into nothing more than light and shadow, and then all they could see was darkness. The floor disappeared from under their feet and they were soon hurtling through space without gravity to hold them down. It felt as though they were being sucked into a giant vacuum cleaner with a force so strong it split apart every atom in their body.

But before either of them had a chance to scream, they were once again standing on solid ground.

The world melted back into existence. They were outside: the cold wind made them shiver and the daylight was bright.

Felix looked around and smiled. 'We're here – 1943.'

5
Rations

'I guess your razor-sharp memory failed you this time, Felix,' Missy said with a scowl. She swept her arms around and pointed to the buildings surrounding them. 'This does not look like an RAF airbase to me.'

The time machine had spat them out in a quiet little village. They were standing on a small green with a cricket pavilion at one end and a duck pond at the other. Houses surrounded the grass, heavy curtains hung in the windows and cars were parked up outside. It was the cars that instantly made Felix realize that the time machine had worked.

Now these are what I call vintage classics! And none of these cars look brand new, he noticed.

They're all a few years old. Which makes sense seeing as all major car manufacturers had their production lines shut down during the war . . . We might not be in an RAF base but we are definitely in another time . . .

The cars didn't look like anything you saw on the road in the present day. They were more box-like, the wheels were thinner and the front bonnets more pronounced.

'Felix, I thought we were travelling to the airbase, not the middle of a village!' Missy said, looking around in bewilderment. 'Someone might have seen us just appear out of thin air.'

Felix gulped down a large mouthful of air. *This is a belly-up failure on a galactic scale!* He scratched his head, trying to think quickly. *The coordinates were right — as if I could ever memorize them incorrectly! Impossible! But maybe . . .*

'I've got it!' Felix's hand shot into the air.

'OK.' Missy looked around. 'Tell me in a minute once we're out of sight of the nosy neighbours.' She pointed at a pair of heavy blackout curtains in a nearby window that were twitching curiously.

'Over there.' Missy pointed and began to run towards a small alleyway between two houses.

As Felix and Missy ran over the village green the sky above them began to thunder with the roar of engines overhead. As they ran they looked up to see five aeroplanes flying low above them. Each plane had white stars painted on its fuselage.

'Enemy aircraft?' Missy shouted back to Felix, her voice tight with concern.

'No,' Felix said with certainty. They stopped running as they reached the little alleyway. With their backs pressed against the alley wall they looked up into the sky and watched the planes descend out of sight.

Einstein poked his head out of Felix's pocket, the scales on his face glowing bright **orange**.

'Don't worry, Einstein,' Felix reassured him. 'You too, Missy. The planes we just saw were American planes. Couldn't you tell by the white stars on the side?'

'I was too busy trying to duck from potential bombs falling from the sky,' Missy said with a frown.

'No need to be so dramatic.' Felix held his hands up apologetically. 'If American planes are flying that low overhead then my guess is that RAF Daws Hill is really close by. I must have memorized the coordinates for the nearest town to the base, not the base itself. All we need to do is ask someone where the base is and then . . .'

'Just walk up to it and get them to let us in?' Missy said incredulously. 'This is wartime, Felix.

57

Don't you think security might be a little bit tighter?'

'OK, so we'll figure out a way to get into the base that doesn't involve the guards opening the doors to us . . .'

'It would have been a lot easier if we could have just time travelled back into the actual base.' Missy folded her arms over her chest.

'Oh, I'm sorry.' Felix mirrored Missy's body language, folding his own arms. 'Is my time machine not good enough for you? Is breaking the natural laws of space and time not enough to—'

Einstein leaped out of Felix's pocket on to the ground between them. His scales were shimmering a deeply unhappy **blue**, and the expression on his face was defiant.

'Einstein's right,' Missy said, her arms dropping to her sides. After two months together in a Roman gladiator school, she could read the lizard's colours as well as Felix. 'We're back in 1943 and we shouldn't be arguing. We should find a way to get to the airbase and get in there before anyone notices us.' She looked down at her T-shirt, blue jeans and Converse trainers and muttered, 'Did we learn nothing from our time in Ancient Rome? We really should have put on some kind of World War Two disguise before coming here.'

She's right, Felix admitted silently to himself. **Although I don't want to say that out loud. Next time we time travel we need to change our clothes first. Next time?! What am I thinking? This is the last time we ever do this!**

'It's too late to worry about that now,' Felix said, as he walked further down the alleyway. 'Let's just get into the base and figure out a disguise then.'

The alleyway led on to a busy street.

Felix and Missy peered around the corner and watched people walk past in a hurry. People of all ages were practically running down the street towards a large queue that was forming in front of a small shop.

A group of three women walked past and Felix and Missy quickly ducked back to avoid being seen. The women wore knee-length skirts and jackets that were cinched in at the waist. Their hair had been set into waves and then pinned against their heads. The three women were wearing small hats, and in their hands they each clutched dog-eared little books. Felix squinted his eyes and just about made out the words 'Ration Book' printed on the front.

Felix tried to remember everything he knew about wartime ration books . . .

※ Before the war, Great Britain imported more than seventy per cent of its food from other countries.

※ It was one of the enemy's key battle strategies to destroy ships bringing food into the UK.

※ To stop people starving to death, the Ministry of Food introduced rationing.

※ Everyone had a ration book, which had coupons for foods like chocolate, eggs, meat and fruit.

※ You could use your coupons to buy food from shops.

※ It didn't matter if you were rich or poor – everyone had the same number of ration coupons.

'They must all be queuing up for their weekly rations,' Missy whispered, peering out into the street.

'Look at them running,' Felix said, pointing. 'You'd think they hadn't eaten in a week!'

Another woman walked past. She was holding the hand of a young boy who was carrying a toy aeroplane. He held the little plane up and moved it through the air, making soaring and roaring sounds as if it was really travelling through the sky. The woman caught sight of someone ahead of her, let go of the small boy's hand and ran ahead. 'Doris!' she called. A lady halfway down the snaking queue in the street turned around and gave a broad smile.

'Pst!' Missy whispered in the direction of the small boy who'd been left alone on the pavement. 'Pst!'

He turned around and looked at her, blinking in confusion.

'Come here,' she said, beckoning him. 'Don't let your mum see.'

'She's not my . . .' the boy said loudly.

'Shhh!' Missy put her fingers to her lips.

The boy came closer, standing at the entrance to the alleyway and looking in at Felix and Missy. He was wearing a smart jacket, shirt and tie, shorts cut off above the knee and socks pulled up above his shins. 'She's not my mother,' the boy whispered. 'She's just looking after me for a bit.'

'Why?' Felix asked without thinking.

He felt Missy kick him hard in the shins and he knew exactly why. *Nice one, atom-brain! This is wartime. Maybe his parents are away fighting. Maybe they're missing in action. Maybe they're dead . . .*

'My mother and father live in London,' the boy said brightly. 'Mummy says it's too dangerous for me there at the moment. Hitler's been dropping his bombs on the city again. Mummy says Hitler is really clumsy and sometimes drops bombs on little boys' houses so it's not safe for me there. So I have to come and live here with her friend for a while.'

'Your mother's right,' Missy agreed. 'Much safer for you here.'

'And you like planes?' Felix pointed to the small tin plane in his hand.

The boy nodded and smiled widely.

'I bet you can tell us where the RAF base is around here.'

'Of course,' the boy replied. 'It's the other end of town.' He pointed behind him, beyond the shops and houses they could see. 'And then through the trees.'

'Harry!' The little boy looked around at the sound of his name.

'I have to go,' he said quickly to Felix and Missy. 'We're queuing up for chocolate rations. If I'm good then I can have a whole square to myself without sharing.'

The boy turned around and ran off.

'Chocolate rations – that explains all the rush,' Missy realized, whispering under her breath.

'Let's hope they're too preoccupied with chocolate to notice us running around dressed in jeans and trainers. Come on, buddy.' Felix picked Einstein off the wall where he'd blended himself into the brick. He carefully put his pet lizard back into his pocket. 'On the count of three we run out of here, across the road and between those two shops over there.' Felix pointed to another alleyway on the opposite side of the road. 'We run in a straight line until we're out of the town, then hopefully we'll be at the base. Ready?' Missy smiled and nodded. 'One . . . two . . . three . . .'

The two friends darted out of the alleyway; they sped across the pavement and into the road, pausing only to make sure no cars were coming. They didn't stop to look around and see if anyone had noticed them. They ran down another alley and out into a small residential street. Smoke was billowing from chimneys and front doors were opening and closing as people were going out with their ration books in their hands and excited smiles on their faces.

People are way too interested in chocolate to worry about us, Felix realized, as they ran between the houses, further away from the shops and out of the town.

Soon Felix could see trees in the distance. *That's where we need to go . . .*

He ran for the trees, with Missy close behind him.

The woods seemed to stretch on ahead of them for miles. *Is this really the right way?* Just as he was about to stop running and question their direction the trees began to thin out and he could see a flash of grey concrete ahead of them.

Jumping Jupiter, that's it! That's the airbase!

A smile crept on to Felix's face as he ran towards the airbase, surrounded by wire fencing.

He allowed himself to stop and catch his breath; he sank to his knees and looked up at the impossibly high walls.

He gasped for breath. 'We're here!'

Missy nodded and rasped, 'We are. Now all we need to do is break in . . .'

6
Spies

Einstein poked his head out of Felix's trouser pocket and frowned up at the tall wire fencing in front of them. It was taller than a three-storey house, and the top was covered in rusted barbed wire.

'We have two options,' Missy stated. 'Option one, we talk our way in at the gate. And option two . . .'

Felix reached into his bag and pulled out a length of super-strong rope.

'We climb over,' Felix said, finishing Missy's sentence. 'Let's head over there.' He pointed towards a section of the wall that was made of brick. 'That'll be easier to climb and we're less likely to get caught. But we need to do this quickly, before someone sees. They don't have CCTV in 1943 but they do have guards, and guards have guns.' They quickly ran towards the bricked section of wall. Felix threw the rope towards the sky and watched as it got tangled up in the barbed wire at the top.

Felix tugged on the rope to check it was secure before he started to climb. *This is about as safe as a cyanide smoothie. Why did I let Missy talk me into this? Oh yes, to prove that aliens didn't abduct Archie . . .*

'Hold on, buddy,' Felix said to Einstein with a nervous smile. 'We're going up . . .'

Felix began to climb the rope with his hands, as his feet walked their way up the tall airbase wall. He was gripping the rope so hard his fingers were white. *Don't look down . . . don't look down . . .* he repeated to himself as he climbed higher and higher. His legs were shaking and his fingers quickly grew numb. He was aware of the ground below and Missy getting further and further away as he climbed.

Finally he reached the top of the towering wall. Clutching the rope between his thighs, he reached down and pulled his jumper off and over his head. He clambered on to the wall's ledge, and threw the jumper over the rusted sharp wire, careful not to stab himself. Slowly, holding his breath, Felix climbed up, sat on his jumper and peered over the top. Beyond the barbed wire he could see a vast airbase with huge aircraft hangars, rows of aeroplanes lined up by the runway and dozens of other small outbuildings and offices. Everywhere he looked there were men in uniform walking about, guns holstered by their sides.

It would have been easier to sneak into a viper's nest than a wartime military base . . .

There were guard towers along the perimeter wall, but thankfully they were nowhere near the spot that Felix had climbed up. *If we climb down the wall and into the base quickly, then we might just make it.* He waved down at Missy and threw the rope back to her. 'Come on up – be quick!'

Missy climbed the rope behind Felix and soon they were both at the top of the wall. He then threw the length of rope over the other side of the wall and began to abseil down. Once again he didn't look down, or stop to think about who might see him and shoot him dead on the spot.

Missy was hot on Felix's heels, and when they both stood on solid ground inside the base she turned to him and said, 'The rope's tangled up in the barbed wire. How are we meant to get it down? We can't just leave it there – people will know we've broken into the base.'

Felix reached into his bag again. 'One of the first things I did when I got Einstein as a pet,' he told Missy, 'was study the chemical composition of his scales and recreate their basic properties in my bedroom laboratory.' Einstein nodded at the memory. 'I used what I'd created to make this –' He held up the can of camouflage spray. Missy frowned, confused. 'Good job I packed it! Look . . .'

Felix sprayed the rope and it instantly turned the same colour as the wall.

'That's impressive,' Missy said.

Felix sprayed upward until the whole rope was covered in camouflage spray. 'There,' he said proudly, putting the can of camouflage spray back into his bag. 'Unless someone comes along and touches the spot of wall where the rope is dangling down, they'll never know it's there.'

'And it means we have a way to escape from the airbase quickly if we have to,' Missy pointed out.

'Exactly,' Felix agreed. 'But the camouflage spray doesn't work that well on human skin, so unless we want someone to see us we need to hide.'

They looked around – there was a small outbuilding to their left.

'Let's take cover in there,' Felix said, pointing at the building. 'Then we'll figure out what we need to do next.'

The door to the small building was open. They ran towards it, their skin prickling with worry at the thought of being caught.

But amazingly no one saw them, and they made it without being caught. They dived inside. It was dark. Only one dull bulb flickered in a windowless corridor. A heavy, musty stench crept up their nose and made them gag as they walked down the dimly lit corridor. It stank of smelly socks, unwashed armpits and grease. It was eerily silent.

'There's no one in here,' Felix whispered. He reached for a door handle along the corridor, pushed it open slowly and peered in. He found a light switch on the wall and flicked it on. The room was empty too. They were standing in what looked like a locker area. Dirty flight suits hung from pegs on the walls, and old boots had been kicked off and scattered all over the floor.

'Here, put this on . . .' Felix grabbed a nearby suit from a peg and tossed it at Missy.

'Rank,' she muttered, pinching her nose in disgust as she stepped into it. 'You know, Felix, just once I would like to time travel somewhere where we could actually wear nice disguises – maybe the court of Louis the Sixteenth or somewhere with fancy dresses. So far we've disguised ourselves in tatty Roman togas, and now stinking pilot uniforms. Gross.'

Felix frowned. 'Who cares if the flight suits smell if they keep us alive?' *Trumpeting tornadoes, Missy is so hard to please!*

Felix put on a flight suit himself. *Actually, this does whiff worse than that new strain of mould I've been cultivating under my bed!*

He held Einstein near to the pocket so that he could climb in. Einstein pinched his little reptilian nose, and was just about to step into the pocket when he did a double take. He reached into the pocket and pulled out a slip of paper that was sitting inside. He gripped the paper between his paws and held it towards Felix.

'Thanks, buddy,' Felix said, taking the piece of paper. 'I wonder what you've found? It looks like a telegram . . .'

MAY 1 1943

AM 8000

AIR 83/122/816

YOU HAVE BEEN SELECTED TO PREPARE FOR A TOP-SECRET MILITARY MISSION STOP THE MISSION IS BEING PLANNED BY WINSTON CHURCHILL HIMSELF STOP THIS COMMAND COMES FROM A SECRET BUNKER STOP AWAIT FURTHER INSTRUCTIONS STOP AIR CHIEF MARSHAL

Missy peered over Felix's shoulder. 'What does it mean?'

'It means that whoever this flight suit belongs to has been selected to prepare for a top-secret mission that's being planned by Winston Churchill himself.' Felix looked over the telegram once again, impressed. 'This could be Bill's flight suit, you know. He was selected to take part in a top-secret test mission, wasn't he?'

Missy took the telegram out of Felix's hands, read over it again and nodded her head in agreement before handing it back to him.

I better not lose this, Felix thought, putting the telegram safely back into the pocket where he'd found it.

'Do you think we've done the right thing?' Missy asked quietly. 'By coming back here?'

Felix thought before he spoke. 'World War Two isn't child's play. Millions of people lost their lives. There's a reason all Bill wants to talk about is dancing with pretty girls and mysterious plane crashes when he talks about the war – everything else must just be too awful to remember. But we came back here with a job to do – to find out what happened to Archie. Let's focus on that and try not to get in the way of any top-secret missions.'

Missy nodded. 'Good idea.' She pointed at a small window on the other side of the room. 'I can see bomber planes outside.'

'Let's sneak over and check them out,' Felix said, excited.

Just as they were leaving the room Felix spotted two oil-stained baseball caps hanging from pegs. 'Here, put this on.' He tossed one to Missy. 'Try to hide your hair in it.'

Missy did her best to contain her wild blonde hair in the dirty cap, but a few loose strands escaped and fell around her face.

They both headed outside again, disguised as best they could in their flight suits and baseball caps. The suits were designed for grown men, so they both had to roll up the arms and legs in order to fit into them.

There were dozens of other men in uniforms scattered around the airfield. Every one of them was busy. Some were refuelling planes, others were checking cockpit controls and tyre pressure. Felix and Missy tried their best to keep their heads down and walk across the airfield unnoticed. They were shorter than everyone else out there, and Missy's rebellious blonde curls would give away the fact that she was a girl if anyone paid too much attention.

I really need to work on my camouflage spray formula so it'll cover skin . . . Felix thought to himself.

Felix charged across the tarmac towards a shiny light bomber aircraft that was sitting unattended.

The small plane was gunmetal grey. Inside the glass cockpit were two seats, one in front of the other. ***The pilot sits at the front and the co-pilot sits behind him,*** Felix realized. Sharp propeller blades sat on the plane's nose, as well as to the front of each wing. A white star in a circle was emblazoned across the side of the plane.

'I wonder if this is like the plane Archie is going to fly off in?' Missy wondered aloud.

Felix shook his head, walking straight up to it. 'It's unlikely. There must be hundreds of planes on the airbase.' He noticed a hose sticking out of the wing of the plane. The hose stretched into the distance and connected to a large tanker parked outside an aircraft hangar. *That looks like a fuel bowser,* thought Felix.

Like everything, Felix had a basic knowledge of World War Two bomber planes. He knew all the major facts:

※ *Light bomber aircraft are usually single-engine planes.*

※ *In World War Two the planes took a payload of around 500–1,000kg.*

※ *These planes evolved as World War Two progressed, producing fighters of greater performance, speed and defensive capability.*

※ *Today the term 'light bomber' isn't used – instead we say 'attack aircraft' or 'strike fighters'.*

But there's so much I don't know, Felix thought to himself, looking up at the plane. *What does it feel like to fly one of these things? How easy is it to land one? Oh, winking wormholes! If there's anything I hate, it's unanswered questions . . .*

'What are you thinking?' Missy asked suspiciously.

'I need to get a closer look at this bad boy . . .'

'Hey, you two!' came an American voice from behind them. 'What do you think you're doing?'

Felix and Missy spun around to see a tall man in a flight suit running over the tarmac towards them. He had slicked over dark blond hair and well-polished shoes, and something about him looked remarkably familiar. As he ran closer, Felix recognized the young man instantly.

'Gaga Bill!' Missy gasped just loud enough for Felix to hear her.

Black holes and comet tails, what is the mathematical probability of running into Bill?

'Who are you?' the young man demanded. 'And what are you doing by my plane?'

'Wh-who are we?' Felix stuttered nervously. 'Who are you?!'

'I'm Flight Lieutenant Bill Hudson of the First Eight,' Bill replied, crossing his arms over his chest. 'And you have exactly thirty seconds to explain who you are and what you're doing tampering with this aircraft before I call over the colonel and have you both locked up in a cell!'

'We're not tampering,' Felix said quickly.

'What are you doing then?' Bill pressed them.

'W-we're, umm . . .' Felix faltered. 'We were just, errr . . . We're here to check the fuel – that's it, yes! We're fuel specialists and we're here to check this aircraft's fuel supply.' Felix walked over and grabbed the hose that was sticking out of the side of the plane.

Bill's eyebrows rose and he gave Felix a very sceptical look. 'You look just like a couple of kids to me.'

'Hey!' Felix tried to sound annoyed. 'We have stunted growth from all the food rationing!'

Bill looked over his shoulder behind him, as if he was looking for someone to call over. *Food rationing? Stunted growth? Why did I say that? Busted!* Felix could feel Missy tense up beside him. *I should have let her do the speaking; Missy's always better than I am at sweet-talking . . .*

But Missy seemed to have lost her tongue completely. Seeing Gaga Bill had robbed her of the ability to say anything.

Felix looked back at the plane and tried to think of something better to say. Nothing came to him. 'Yep, we're vertically challenged fuel specialists. Not children – oh no. Just going to give this bad boy one more thorough check –' Felix took hold of the hose – 'to see if it's fuelling up just like it's . . .'

But as Felix tugged on it the hose fell out of the

wing of the plane and started to spray watery green liquid everywhere.

Felix, Missy and Bill were quickly splattered in stinking fuel. The hose pumped the fuel out on to the tarmac at an alarming rate and soon a large pool had gathered around them.

'What is going on over here?!' came an angry voice.

An older man with a large grey moustache and several golden stars on the shoulders of his uniform came charging angrily towards them.

'Colonel, I can explain exactly what's going on,' Bill said quickly, trying to wipe the petrol from his face.

'I should hope so!' the older man replied. 'Who are these children?'

Felix began to argue. 'We're not children, we're—'

'I don't know, sir,' Bill replied, cutting Felix off and giving him an angry look.

The colonel scowled at Bill and clenched his fists. 'Whoever they are you've just stood there and watched as they tried to sabotage one of our aircraft!'

'No, sir,' Bill tried to protest.

'Silence, Hudson!' the colonel screamed at him.
'You know how important these planes are to us.
How delicate our preparation for the mission ahead
is. For all we know these children could be spies
sent by Hitler to uncover our secrets and sabotage
our planes!'

'We're not spies!' Felix shouted, but this only seemed to make the colonel even angrier.

'Typical Hitler!' the colonel seethed. 'Sending kids in to do his dirty work. Doesn't have the guts to do it himself. He'll be sending in puppy dogs and hamsters next!'

'We do not work for Hitler!' Missy shouted, suddenly finding her voice.

'Explain that to a military court!' the colonel bellowed. In no time at all ten other men in flight suits had gathered around them and Missy and Felix had been rounded up. Felix felt someone twist his arms behind his back. And out of the corner of his eye he saw someone pull Missy's baseball cap off and reveal her head of blonde hair beneath.

The guards ripped Felix's backpack from his shoulders and tossed it through the air. It landed at the colonel's feet with a thud. 'My bag!' Felix screamed.

'My bag now.' The colonel smirked back, picking up the bag and slinging it over his shoulder. 'Guards, search them!'

In the name of Charles Darwin, I HAVE to get my bag back! My camouflage spray, my hologram machine, my radio equipment, the time machine remote control . . . the time machine remote control! If I don't get it back, then we'll be stuck in 1943 forever!

Felix felt a heavy hand dive into his flight-suit pocket and immediately pull out the telegram he'd found in there before.

'I found this, sir,' the guard said, handing over the telegram to the colonel.

The colonel quickly scanned the contents of the telegram, his moustache twitching in rage and his face turning as red as a beetroot.

He looked up at Felix. 'You're a spy,' he accused him through gritted teeth. 'You came here to uncover our secrets – we won't let you leave here alive to feed information back to the enemy. And you too, Lieutenant Hudson!' He turned to Bill. 'Why didn't you arrest these two as soon as you saw them? Are you working with them? Or are you too dumb to realize that we have two spies in our midst? Either way you'll spend the night in the cells, and I'm stripping you of your privileges until further notice!'

'No, sir!' Bill tried to argue.

'You two are spies. Child spies but spies none the less,' the colonel spat at Felix and Missy. 'And you –' he turned to Bill – 'you have been fraternizing with spies. Lock them all up!' he commanded the guards. 'Lock them all up without food and water – we'll see what it takes to make them talk . . .'

7

Holograms

The heavy cell door slammed shut behind them.

For the love of all things atomic! Me, Missy and Bill all locked up in a cell! This was not how the plan was meant to play out . . .

Bill sank to his knees and held his head in his hands. 'My career – my life – hanging in the balance. Everything could be ruined, just because I ran over to stop a couple of kids messing with my plane.'

'We're going to help you get out of here and clear your name,' Missy said, trying to reassure Bill. 'I promise.'

'The colonel's right – for all I know you two are enemy spies sent in here to scout out our secrets and sabotage our plans. What is it Hitler wants to know, huh? What we give our fighter pilots for breakfast? Why we all look so good-looking in oil-stained flight suits? How we comb our hair each morning? As if Hitler has enough brain cells to want to know something that's actually important!'

'We've already told you,' Missy argued. 'We don't work for Hitler!'

Bill rose to his feet and pointed an angry finger at Missy. 'And if you're not a spy – whoever you are – I'm holding you personally responsible for putting my career, everything I've ever worked for, into jeopardy. The First Eight need me to fly planes and help win this war – how am I going to do that when I'm locked up in a bunker?!'

Jeez, now I know where Missy gets her dramatic streak!

'Look, please calm down,' Felix said to Bill. 'The colonel said you're having your privileges stripped, but what does that mean?'

'Calm down?!' Bill screamed. 'No privileges means no radio, no playing cards with the guys or making telephone calls back home, and no going to the dance at the village hall tonight. I've been looking forward to that all week,' he added sulkily.

Missy pulled Felix aside and spoke quietly so Bill couldn't hear. 'He must be talking about the dance he met Great-Grandma Stella at,' she said, wide-eyed. 'He's right – he can't go if he's locked up in here with us. And if he doesn't go then he'll never meet Stella. If he never meets Stella then he'll never fall in love, never get married, never have a son, never have a granddaughter and never have a great-granddaughter – do you see what I'm saying, Felix? I might never even be born!' Missy hadn't stopped for breath – she took in a big gasp.

'Missy,' Felix said, rolling his eyes. 'You and Bill are as dramatic as each other. Calm down! I'm going to find a way to fix this.'

'Good!' Missy frowned, thinking deeply. 'Felix, maybe we should go home now.'

'What do you mean?' he asked.

'I mean that if being here risks my never being born then I think we should just fire up the time machine and go back to your bedroom.'

'Missy, do I need to point out the obvious?' Felix said, annoyed. Missy gave him a blank look with her big blue eyes. 'My backpack was taken away by the guards! Even if we wanted to go home right this second and leave Bill banged up in a cell we can't. Not without the time machine remote control.'

Missy's hands flew to her face in horror. 'Felix! I was so busy screaming and kicking at the guards I didn't even notice they'd taken your bag. What are we going to do?'

'We're going to get it back,' Felix said resolutely. 'Bill?' He turned to Bill, who had his head in his hands. 'We need you to trust us.'

'And why should I do that?' Bill muttered.

'Because right now you don't have much choice,' Felix replied. 'And if I were your enemy, would I know that your name is Bill Hudson and you grew up in Virginia and you learned to fly planes when you were not much older than I am now?'

Bill looked up at Felix, startled. 'Who knows what kind of information a spy has access to?'

'We're your friends,' Missy said earnestly. 'Not enemies.'

'A spy could know that information about me,' Bill said, frowning.

'Would they know that your best friend is Archie, and you grew up together and liked the same baseball cards and ice-cream flavours? You learned to fly planes at the same time and when you signed up to fight in the US Air Force you were both assigned to the Eight Bomber Command?'

Bill was speechless.

KNOCK. KNOCK. KNOCK.

The three of them spun around and stared at the cell door.

KNOCK. KNOCK. KNOCK.

A voice came from the other side of the door. 'Bill?'

'Archie?' Bill answered.

Felix and Missy looked at one another and said in unison, 'Archie!'

'Buddy, what are you doing here?' Bill moved towards the door, speaking in animated whispers to his best friend standing behind it. 'You gotta help me out here. I mean, come on, I'm not a spy!'

'I know that,' Archie reassured him from behind the door. 'When I heard what had happened I came straight over. I offered to guard you – as if I was gonna let anyone else do it! Don't worry, buddy, I'm gonna get you outta here. Tomorrow's the test flight, remember?'

'How can I forget?' Bill replied, closing his eyes and shaking his head in frustration. 'I gotta be there to take my plane up and try her out.'

'I hear ya, buddy,' came Archie's voice.

'Er, I hate to interrupt . . .' Felix said. Bill spun

around and blinked in surprise, as if he'd forgotten Felix and Missy were even there. 'But do you think Archie could do me a BIG favour?'

'Was that one of the spies speaking?' said Archie, from the other side of the cell door. 'Bill, don't trust a word he—'

'They're kids, Archie,' Bill said quickly. 'I don't know who they are. But they know a load of stuff about me, and about you too – like how we grew up together and liked the same baseball cards.'

'A spy could know those things,' said Archie, sounding sceptical.

'I don't know . . .' Bill said, staring at Missy and chewing his lip in thought. 'There's something about these kids that I want to trust. They seem . . . familiar. You remember in basic flight training we were always told to trust our gut instincts?'

'I remember,' Archie replied.

'Well, my gut is telling me that these are two kids who just wanna help. Maybe they're going about it the wrong way but I think we can trust them.'

Thank the cosmos! Bill is on our side!

Felix ran towards the cell door and said to Archie, 'You can trust us. We're here to help you. I promise.'

'I don't know if I trust you,' Archie said slowly, 'but I trust Bill, and if he wants to trust you then I will too. But if you're leading us into trouble then I will personally be the one to have you shot at dawn. You understand?'

Shot at dawn, thought Felix with panic. **A traitor's execution!**

'We're not traitors or spies or enemies,' Felix said. 'I'll find a way to prove it, I promise. But first I need you to do something for me.'

'What?' Archie asked.

Felix took a deep breath. 'I need you to find the bag that the colonel took from me and bring it back here.'

'No way!' Felix could hear Archie splutter. 'It's worth more than my life to go hunting around . . .'

'Exactly!' Felix said quickly. 'It is worth more than . . . well, maybe not more than your life. But it's worth a great deal. And I can't help Bill if I don't have my bag.'

Felix stared Bill in the eye, and Bill stared back before slowly turning to the door and saying, 'Archie, let's do it, let's trust him.'

'OK,' Archie agreed. Felix and Missy punched the air and high-fived each other. 'But if I can't do it, or I bring it back here and you've tricked us then you're on your own. As good as dead. Shot at dawn. Understand?'

'Yes,' Felix and Missy both said together.

They heard Archie's footsteps echo along the corridor outside as he walked away.

'So what's the plan?' Bill said, wide-eyed and excited. 'You have something in that bag that proves who you are? Proves you're not spies?'

'Not exactly,' said Felix. 'I have something in that bag that's going to help us break out.'

'I can't break out!' Bill said, horrified. 'If I run away then they'll think I'm guilty for sure. I need to stick around and clear my name!'

'What if I told you I knew a way for us to all sneak out of the cell for a few hours – without anyone knowing? We'd be back before anyone realized we were gone.'

Bill narrowed his eyes. 'I don't know . . .'

'I promise you, you won't regret it,' Felix said.

Before Bill could say another word the cell door creaked open.

A worried face poked around the door, shortly followed by a slim body and an extended arm holding Felix's backpack.

'My bag!' Felix snatched it off Archie and started rummaging through it.

Missy smiled at Archie. 'That was quick!'

'The colonel left it on his office desk. He's gone out to dinner – all I had to do was go in there and take it.'

'Ah-ha!' Felix pulled out a small wooden box from the bag. It looked like an old-fashioned camera. There were buttons on the top and a lens at the front.

'Felix, what's that?' Missy asked.

One of my finest inventions to date . . .

'This,' Felix said proudly, 'is a homemade hologram machine. And it's our ticket out of here.'

Felix turned the machine on and pointed the lens at Bill. He clicked down on one of the buttons at the top, as if he were taking a photo.

Bill moved away from the door, his eyes fixed on the strange object in Felix's hands. 'What did you say it was?'

Felix smiled. 'Just watch this . . .'

Felix pressed down on another button at the top of the box and pointed the box's lens at the far wall. A 3D hologram of Bill projected into the air.

Missy whooped in delight. 'A hologram!'

'That's me! How in the world did you . . . ?' Bill moved towards the hologram and tried to touch it, his hand passing through light and air.

'That's a hologram of you,' Felix replied.

Hologram:

* A 3D photographic recording of an object using a laser.

* A hologram is recorded using information of the light that surrounds every angle of an object. Therefore it can be viewed from every angle, not just face-on like a photograph.

* A hologram is different from a normal photograph because it needs to be taken by a laser, and can then be viewed in 3D. A hologram is the most accurate 3D image in the world – it looks very lifelike, almost as if the object were right in front of you!

* You don't need special glasses or lenses to see holograms.

'I captured your image a minute ago in the hologram machine. And the machine projects a life-size image out of this lens here. I made the machine myself. I've programmed it to encode laser light fields with images taken through this lens.'

He pointed to the lens at the front of the box. 'It's a clever piece of equipment; it relies on the optical phenomena of interference and diffraction.'

'Excuse Felix,' Missy said to Bill. 'He gets quite technical when he's talking about science.'

'This is incredible,' Bill whispered, amazed by the image of himself projected into thin air. 'If this is the technology the enemy have then we're . . .'

'We're not the enemy,' Felix said firmly.

'Say I do trust you,' said Bill, 'where are you planning to take me?'

'I'll explain on the way,' Felix said, looking to Archie. 'Here –' He handed him a walkie-talkie from his bag. 'This is one half of a radio. I've got the other half. If you need to contact us, if anyone notices we're gone – then radio me straightaway.'

Archie's face was as white as a sheet.

'Is there anyone else out there?' Felix pointed beyond the door. 'Can you sneak us out?'

Archie looked into the corridor outside and then back into the cell, shaking his head. 'The coast is clear – they're all at the mess hall for dinner.'

Missy turned to Bill. 'It's now or never. Are you with us?'

Bill looked towards the cell door. 'Archie, what do you think?'

'I think a machine that shoots out images like that is worth breaking the rules for,' Archie replied. 'Be back here by twenty-three hundred hours, OK, buddy?'

'OK,' Bill agreed.

Felix quickly took snapshots of himself and Missy with the hologram machine, and set them up to project into the air next to the hologram of Bill. 'If anyone comes looking for us, they'll see the hologram images of us and never suspect we're missing. So long as they don't try to talk to us . . .' Felix muttered.

One by one, Felix, Missy and Bill slipped out of the cell. Archie closed the door behind them and locked it.

'Stay safe, buddy.' Archie gave Bill a quick slap on the back. 'Wherever they're taking you, come back in one piece.'

Bill gave Archie a weak smile and whispered,

'I don't know who these kids are. But whoever they are, our lives are in their hands.'

If only he knew how true that was, thought Felix, overhearing. *And it's not just their lives at stake. He looked over at Missy. If we can't fix this mess, then Missy will never even be born . . .*

8
First Dance

The sun had set and clouds were covering the moon. The darkness helped them make it to the airbase's barbed-wire fence without being seen.

Felix ran his hand along the wall until he felt the rope he'd left camouflaged there only hours before.

'Stay still.' Bill grabbed Felix's collar and began to reach for the pocket at the top of his flight suit. 'There's some kind of lizard in your pocket. Hold still and I'll kill—'

'NO!!' Felix and Missy both shouted at once.

Felix jumped backwards. 'You can't kill lizards! Besides, this isn't any old lizard, it's my pet chameleon Einstein.'

'What kind of kid has a pet lizard in his pocket?' Bill said curiously.

'The kind who also invented a hologram machine,' Missy replied.

'Hey, buddy, you getting hungry?' Felix whispered down at Einstein. The little lizard flashed **purple** for yes. 'Hold on tight – I'll get you some food soon, don't worry. Right now we've got a wall to climb . . .'

Ignoring the confused look on Bill's face, Felix took the camouflaged rope safely in his grasp, and began to climb . . .

Bill turned and watched Felix magically ascend the wall. 'Hey, is that rope . . . ?'

'Camouflaged? Yes,' Missy answered, taking the rope and beginning to climb. 'And yes, Einstein the lizard can communicate with the colour of his scales. There's probably a few things about us that might confuse you. No time for answers though. Hurry up before someone spots us!'

'If you guys aren't spies, then what are you?' Bill whispered in amazement as Missy began to climb the rope after Felix. 'You from the future or something?'

Felix and Missy both heard what Bill said but they stayed very quiet!

I'd rather explain quantum mechanics to a guinea pig than answer that question! Felix thought to himself.

In no time at all Felix, Missy and Bill were the other side of the fence. Einstein scuttled down Felix's leg and on to the ground below. His scales were a worrying shade of orange.

He's right. We're out of the base but we're miles from anywhere. Hale-Bopp's comet! 'How are we going to get into town?' he said aloud.

'Into town?' Bill frowned. 'What do we need to do there? Is there some kind of military official who's going to prove who you are? Prove you're not spies?'

'Not exactly,' Missy said. 'We're taking you to the village dance.'

'WHAT?' Bill exploded in anger. 'You made me break out of the cell to go to a dumb dance?!' Bill took hold of the rope ready to climb back into the RAF base. 'I need to get back in that cell – if I'd have known you were breaking me out to go to a dance . . . !'

'I thought you said you were looking forward to it?' Missy said sheepishly, running after him.

'Yes, but being court-martialled for spying is slightly more important than going to some stupid dance!'

'No it's not!' Missy said through gritted teeth. 'And the dance isn't stupid!'

'What if we told you there was someone at the dance that we needed you to meet?' Felix said quickly, trying to keep the peace. 'Someone important.'

'A military leader?' Bill asked hopefully. 'A politician?'

'Um, no,' Felix admitted. 'But you've trusted us this far. Please trust us just a little bit more?'

Bill gave Felix an exasperated look. 'Fine, but it's too far to walk. There's a bus stop not too far from here though.'

It only took them a few minutes to reach the bus stop. They never stopped looking over their shoulders, convinced that someone from the airbase might be following them, but the bus arrived without event after only a few minutes' wait, and they all hopped on.

When they reached their stop, Missy turned to Bill with a frown. 'We can't let you go to the dance like that,' she said with a tut. 'You look such a state! Your hair's a mess, your uniform's dirty, you smell like petrol . . .'

'Bill! Bill!' someone shouted as they got off the bus. They turned around to see a handsome pilot in a very smart blue uniform walking towards them. 'Bill – it is you! What are you doing here? I heard a story about you having your privileges stripped

– something about two kids spying?' He looked at Felix and Missy suspiciously.

'Hey, Mikey, and no – erm, that's just a rumour. It was all a big misunderstanding,' Bill replied, pushing hair out of his eyes nervously.

'Hey, Mikey?' Missy said. Felix recognized the sparky look in her eyes … . *She's had an idea . . .*

'Nice uniform,' Missy said, smiling.

'Thanks,' Mikey replied, looking down at himself proudly. 'I wanted to look my best for the dance tonight. I heard there'll be a lot of pretty girls there! Hey, Bill, where you off to in your flight suit? You're not going to the dance like that, are you?

'Pff, no.' Bill looked embarrassed. 'Erm, we were just . . .'

'Felix, open your bag,' Missy demanded.

In the name of Newton . . . !

Missy pulled Felix's bag from his shoulder without another word and started to rifle through it.

Felix frowned. 'What are you doing, Missy?'

Everything we need is in there! Not only are we as stuffed as a wormhole without it, if people get one peek in there they'll know there's something fishy about us!

'Here.' Missy pulled out a handful of chocolate bars that Felix had stashed in the bag. 'You won't miss these, will you, Felix?'

'Ermmm . . .'

'I didn't think so.' Missy turned to Mikey. 'Mikey, I know it's pretty hard to get your hands on good-quality chocolate here in England right now, what with chocolate being rationed and everything. Well, in my hands I have a month's supply of chocolate and I'll give it to you right here and now if you do one thing for me.'

Mikey licked his lips. 'What?'

Felix could see in his eyes that Mikey would do anything for the chocolate.

'Bill needs to borrow your suit.'

Half an hour later, Felix, Missy and Bill were standing outside the village hall. The sounds of the dance were already blaring away from inside. It didn't sound like the kind of music Felix and Missy were used to hearing – there were no electronic beats, no rapping or harmonized voices. A steady stream of people were making their way into the dance hall. The women were all in smart skirts and tops with bright red lipstick on their lips and kitten-heel shoes on their feet. Most of the men were in military uniforms, their shoes polished and their hair gelled into neat side partings.

Felix and Missy had scrubbed up as best they could, but they were both still wearing the too-big oil-stained flight suits they'd borrowed from the base.

Felix looked over at Bill, who looked very smart and handsome in the clean, pristine uniform he'd borrowed from Mikey. *One thing Missy Six is*

very good at is thinking on her feet . . . that, and
bribing people!

Inside the dance hall the light was soft and
streamers draped from the ceiling as though
the people dancing were celebrating something
special. A band played up on the stage, and the
singer wore a dress that puffed out at her hips
and had scarlet lipstick on her lips. The music
sounded a bit slow compared to what Felix and
Missy were used to hearing on the radio back
home, but everyone else in the dance hall thought
it was fantastic. Men were swinging girls around
and twirling them about the dance floor. Everyone
was smiling and laughing – you would never have
guessed that there was a war on.

Felix looked up at Bill. His eyes were focused
on something – someone – on the far side of the
room. A dreamy expression filled his face and his
mouth twitched up into a shy smile.

Felix followed his gaze towards a pretty girl
standing on the edge of the dance floor. The girl
had blonde corkscrew curls and big blue eyes.
She looks just like her great-granddaughter,

Felix thought, smiling. The girl was watching the dancers twirl past her and swaying along to the beat of the music.

Stella!

Missy must have seen her too, because before anyone could stop her she ran across the room towards the girl and threw her arms around her.

Oh, flipping fuses and force fields! Can't Missy for once just make things easy for me?!

Felix quickly ran over to pull Missy away from a very confused-looking Stella.

'I'm so sorry,' Missy said, apologizing to Stella, as Felix tore her away. 'It's just that I've always wanted to meet you.'

'May I introduce myself?' said Bill to Stella, standing behind Felix. 'My name's Bill Hudson.'

Stella smiled warmly and shook Bill's hand. 'I'm Stella, it's a pleasure to meet you, Mr Hudson.'

'Please, call me Bill,' he said with a smile. 'Could I have the pleasure of this dance?'

Stella smiled sweetly and nodded, and Bill led her to the dance floor looking like a man who had just won the lottery.

'Phew!' Missy said, wiping her brow dramatically and slumping down on a nearby chair. 'Well, at least that part of history has righted itself again. Now Bill and Stella can fall hopelessly in love and I don't have to worry about never being born.'

Felix sat down next to Missy and watched as Bill and Stella waltzed their way around the dance floor, their eyes never looking away from one another.

This soppy love story is really not what time travel is all about . . .

'Ouch!' Felix reached down towards a sharp pain in his leg. 'Einstein!'

Einstein was digging his claws into Felix's thigh from inside his trouser pocket.

Beside him, Missy's tummy let out a loud and embarrassing growl. 'I'm starving,' she announced.

'So's Einstein,' Felix said. 'Shame you gave away all our chocolate supply!'

'Don't be silly,' Missy laughed, reaching into the pocket of her flight suit. She pulled out three chocolate bars. 'I saved some – one for you, one for me and one for Bill to give to Stella at the end of the night. That way she'll definitely want to see him again.'

'What about Einstein?' Felix asked, realizing how hungry he suddenly was himself.

'He'll have to share with us,' replied Missy, ripping into her chocolate bar and snapping a piece off for Einstein.

They sat and munched on their chocolate, trying to make the bars last as long as they possibly could, and watched Bill and Stella dance.

They danced slow dances, fast dances, jazz and jive dances – Bill and Stella danced all night long until the music stopped and everyone began to leave.

'Can I see you again?' Bill asked Stella, his eyes shining like stars. 'Tomorrow night? There's another dance here – we could go together.'

'How about tomorrow day?' Stella smiled. 'I've never seen the inside of an airbase before. Maybe you could give me a guided tour, and I could see your plane?'

Bill smiled from ear to ear. 'I'd like that very much.'

'Are you forgetting one thing?' Felix pointed out. 'You're meant to be locked . . . ouch!'

Felix bent down and rubbed at the spot on his shin that Missy had kicked.

'Here,' Missy whispered to Bill, elbowing Felix out of the way. She pushed the last chocolate bar into Bill's hands. 'Give Stella this.'

'This is for you.' Bill presented Stella with the chocolate bar. 'So I'll see you tomorrow, at the airbase?'

'Of course,' Stella said, beaming and taking the chocolate from Bill. 'I'll see you then.'

They took the bus back to the airbase. Despite the evening going to plan, Felix was not feeling happy.

Something about this isn't quite right . . .

There was nothing in the story Bill told us about Stella coming to the airbase to look at Bill's plane. But then again, there was also nothing in the story about being arrested and locked up for fraternizing with spies!

Bill stared out of the window, his eyes glazed over with thoughts of Stella. 'This important person we were meant to be meeting at the dance?' he asked dreamily. 'We must have completely forgotten to find them.'

'Don't worry,' Felix reassured him. 'Everything is just as it should be . . .'

Why don't I believe that?

'Missy.' Felix nudged her in the ribs. 'From now

114

on we cannot interfere with anything. I'm worried that we're changing the course of history by being back here.'

'But we could stop Archie going up in that plane,' Missy pointed out. 'Stop him from going missing.'

'NO!' Felix said firmly. 'That would change the course of history. We can't do that. It's our job to find out what happened to Archie, not stop him from flying that plane.'

'OK,' she said. 'Archie still needs to go up in the plane, just like Gaga Bill said he did. And we need to find out why he never came back. But how are we going to do that?'

'I'm not quite sure yet,' Felix admitted. 'A secret camera on the plane maybe? A tracking device in Archie's flight suit? I'm still working on it. One thing I do know for certain is that we are not leaving 1943 until we have solved this mystery. This trip has been too much trouble for it to all be for nothing!'

9
A Familiar Face

Einstein was the first to climb up the camouflaged rope to the top of the airbase's barbed-wire fence.

The little lizard was completely camouflaged as he climbed, but when he reached the top Felix could just about make out his scales changing to a bright **red** in the light of the moon.

Red = danger!

'It's not safe,' Felix whispered to Missy and Bill beside him. 'Good job we sent Einstein up there as a lookout.'

Bill looked up at the position of the stars in the sky. 'It must be nearly midnight,' he said quietly. 'Guards are usually patrolling this section of the airbase wall around now.'

'We can't wait down here all night,' Missy whispered impatiently. 'We're already late. We need to get back into the cell before someone realizes we're gone.'

'Just give it a minute or two,' Bill replied confidently.

Sure enough, a few minutes later the scales on Einstein's back began to glow a soft **purple**.

Purple = yes.

'The coast is clear,' Felix whispered excitedly. Without losing another second, Felix began to scale the rope. Just like before, he didn't stop to look down or think about how high up he was. Once he was at the top, he squeezed himself between the barbed wire. He patted Einstein fondly. 'Nice work, buddy.' Then he waited for Missy and Bill to join him.

On the ground below he could see the military base illuminated by moonlight. There was no sign of patrolling guards. *Who knows how long we have,* he thought to himself. *The sooner we get down and back into that cell, the better . . .*

As soon as Missy and Bill were also at the top of

the fence Felix flung the rope down the other side and prepared to abseil to the ground.

Just as the rope hit the ground below, something in the distance inside the airbase caught his eye.

Great galloping Galileo! It's a guard out on patrol. Black holes and comet tails! This is not what we need!

As the guard moved closer, Felix got a better look. *Hang on a minute . . . something about that guard looks strangely . . .*

'Felix,' Missy whispered in his ear. They were crouching on the top of the fence, and Felix knew they didn't have long to climb down before they were spotted. 'That guard —' She pointed to the man Felix had also spotted. 'He looks just like . . .'

'Professor Aldini,' they both whispered at the same time.

It was safe to say that Aldini, a colleague of Missy's mum at the British Museum, was NOT a friend. Aldini had it in for Professor Six and had made it quite clear that he would stop at nothing to ruin her reputation. He never missed a chance to try to have her fired.

'Shouldn't he be back at the museum chasing after my mum's job and not pacing up and down on an airbase in 1943?' Missy whispered, confused.

'It's not him.' Felix shook his head. 'It can't

be. Professor Aldini hasn't even been born yet, remember?' He spoke quietly, so Bill wouldn't hear. 'Maybe that's his grandfather or something?' Felix shrugged.

'Maybe,' Missy said, not sounding convinced. 'Alien abductions, Bermuda Triangles and now doppelgängers . . . Something about this mystery is not as straightforward as you thought it was, Felix.'

'Missy,' Felix whispered back, annoyed, 'I told you before, Archie was not abducted by—'

'Guys,' Bill said, sounding concerned. 'We gotta get down from this wall or that guard's going to start taking shots at us.'

'We can't climb down with him so near to us – he'll see us straightaway!' Missy said.

'Let's radio Archie,' Bill suggested. 'Maybe he could create a diversion?'

Felix reached into his pocket and pulled out his radio.

'I'll do it.' Bill went to grab the radio from Felix. 'You won't know military radio lingo.'

But before Bill had a chance to take the radio, Felix was already speaking.

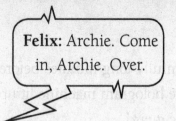

Felix: Archie. Come in, Archie. Over.

Archie: Receiving you clear. Over.

The funny thing about time travelling, Felix thought to himself, looking at Bill, ***is that something rewires in your brain so that you can understand local languages. Not that I'm about to explain time travelling to you.***

'Felix knows a lot of things,' Missy whispered to Bill and shrugged.

Felix: We're stuck at the top of the airbase wall. There's a guard prowling around beneath us. Over.

Archie: I'll create a diversion. Over.

Felix: Use the hologram machine. Go into the cell, take out the machine and point it outside towards the guard. Over.

Archie: Copy that. Out.

They waited a few painfully long minutes before the flash of light from the hologram machine lit up the darkness ahead of the guard.

Please work . . . Please work . . . In the name of the Andromeda Galaxy please work . . .

Felix held his breath and crossed his fingers and toes as he watched hologram images of himself, Missy and Bill project into the night. He could almost feel Einstein glowing orange with worry on his shoulder as he bit his lip and watched.

Come on, Archie . . . move the box around . . . Make it look like we're running away . . .

As if Archie had read Felix's mind, the holograms began to move – it looked as though they were escaping off into the night.

'The prisoners!' The guard shouted so loudly he must have woken half the base up. 'They're running away! Stop them!'

It's working!

The guard began to run off, chasing after the holograms.

'Get down, fast!' Felix instructed.

One after the other, they quickly and carefully

climbed down the rope and were soon running through the airbase towards the building they were supposed to be locked up in.

'Get in,' Archie said, as soon as he saw them. He held the cell door open and they ran inside. 'I can't keep the guards away much longer. Pretty soon they're going to realize they're chasing after nothing and . . .'

'They're coming!' Bill said, hearing footsteps in the distance.

Archie slammed the cell door shut with Felix, Missy and Bill once again locked behind it.

No sooner had it slammed shut, the cell door began to swing open again.

Felix immediately took off his backpack and threw it on to the floor. He sat down on top of it and, seeing that he was trying to hide it, Missy quickly sat down next to him, making sure the bag was completely out of sight.

The cell door flew wide open and a red-faced guard stood in the doorway.

As the guard stormed into the light of the cell, Felix's jaw dropped open at the sight of him.

Well, push me through a wormhole and call me 'Jupiter'! He really, really does look like Professor Aldini from the museum.

The guard was tall and slim with slick black hair. Behind round thick-framed glasses his dark eyes burned with fury. His fists clenched and trembled by his sides and his bottom lip quivered with rage.

'Can you tell me why I've just chased after you and watched you disappear right in front of me?' the familiar-looking guard asked through gritted teeth.

Felix shrugged, trying not to show how out of breath he was from running through the airbase as he said, 'We don't know what you're talking about. We've been here since yesterday.'

'Archie?' the guard asked. 'Is he telling the truth?'

'Not one word of a lie,' Archie said. 'They've been in here the whole time. I've been guarding the door myself.'

'Well, make sure they stay here,' the guard snarled. 'The colonel wants to speak to Hudson in the morning. Oh, and you wouldn't happen to know what's happened to the prisoners' bag, would you?'

'I don't know what you mean,' Archie shrugged innocently.

'It's gone missing from the colonel's office. He's not happy. We need to find it.'

Felix held his breath, feeling the backpack underneath his bottom. *Please don't ask us to stand up, please don't ask us to stand up . . .*

The guard narrowed his eyes at Felix, but without another word he turned around and left.

125

The cell door slammed shut once again and Felix, Missy and Bill were alone in the cell.

Bill slumped down on the ground. 'I suppose I should be worried about standing in front of the colonel tomorrow. But all I can think about is Stella, and seeing her again.'

'All right, Romeo,' Felix said. 'Whatever happens tomorrow we need to try to get some rest. I don't know about you but a bar of chocolate for dinner hasn't exactly filled me up and if we're going to figure out a way to get out of this cell, see Stella, clear our names *and* make sure the mission tomorrow goes ahead as planned then we need to get some rest.'

'Good idea, Felix,' Missy agreed.

It didn't take long before Missy and Bill were snoring away on the cold cell floor.

Felix was exhausted but couldn't sleep. His mind was buzzing with all the facts and questions from the day . . .

The story's not playing out like old Bill said it would . . . Things are changing . . . history's changing . . . that can't be a good thing.

> ✳ *How are we going to get out of this cell without being caught?*
>
> ✳ *How are we going to clear Bill's name?*
>
> ✳ *Why does that guard look SO much like Aldini?*
>
> ✳ *I am SO hungry! I wonder if I can find a way to get my hands on a ration book . . .*

Einstein came and sat on Felix's chest as he lay down; he was a very glum shade of blue.

'Don't worry, Einstein, there's no need to be sad,' Felix said quietly. 'I'll find a way to fix everything. Right now I wish I could take my mind off things . . . I need a distraction.'

Einstein waddled down towards Felix's pocket and tapped his foot on the radio antenna that was sticking out.

Felix smiled, pulling the radio out of his pocket. 'You're right, I could use the radio to tap into the airwaves. Listen in to some of the messages flying around tonight. That's bound to distract me!'

Felix twiddled with the radio's knobs until the static turned into a beeping sound. There were short beeps and long beeps.

'It's Morse code!' Felix announced. 'Awesome, I know how to translate that!'

Felix reached into his bag and pulled out a pencil and paper. He began to write down the Morse code he heard.

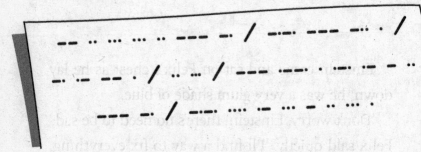

Mission code name is Operation Chastise

'Operation Chastise!' Felix sat bolt upright, his heart pounding. 'I know what that is!'

Einstein flashed **purple** for 'Yes' – he wanted to know more.

'It's the Dam Busters mission – one of the most famous military operations of the whole war!'

10
Dam Busters

The Dam Buster Mission – the facts:

❀ **Code name:** Operation Chastise

❀ **Mission:** Destroy enemy dams

❀ **When:** 16–17 May 1943

❀ **What:** British and Commonwealth bomber planes dropped specially developed bouncing bombs.

❀ **Fact:** Nineteen aircraft took part in the mission, but only eleven planes returned.

Felix barely slept a wink all night. The facts of the Dam Busters mission had run through his head on a loop while the others snored away around him.

Archie's plane won't even get to take part in the mission. He'll disappear on the test flight . . . Maybe that's why no Americans took part in the mission for real after what happened to Archie . . .

The cell door swung open just after dawn, and a guard threw down a prisoners' breakfast of stale bread and suspicious-smelling water at their feet.

It was the same guard they'd seen last night.

As he stood in the doorway Felix got another good long look at his face.

He's the spitting image of Aldini — he must be a relative of his, must be. But wait . . . ?

Felix had noticed a deep red scar running across the back of the guard's right hand. *I wonder how he got that? Looks nasty . . .*

'Sleep well?' the guard said with a knowing smirk to Felix.

Felix sat up and stretched out his sore limbs. The hard cell floor was not the best place to get a good night's sleep. 'I've slept better,' he replied.

'I'm sure you're used to fine mattresses and duck-down quilts,' the guard said with a cruel snarl. 'You'd better forget all about them and get used to the cold hard ground. There'll be no creature comforts where you end up when you're found guilty of spying.'

'We're not spies!' Felix said emphatically.

'We'll see about that,' the guard said. 'Your hearing with the colonel is this afternoon.'

Without another word, the guard turned on his heel and left, slamming the heavy cell door behind him.

Einstein had been camouflaged into the wall, but as soon as the guard had left the small lizard sprinted across the floor towards the plates of food. He pulled his lip down and turned his scales **green** in disgust as he poked at the stale bread with one of his feet.

'Where's Archie?' Missy asked, turning her nose up as she took a whiff of the water.

'He'll be off shift now,' Bill said, hungrily biting into a chunk of stale bread. 'With any luck he'll be selected to take my place on the test flight this afternoon. I don't trust anyone else to fly my plane apart from him.'

Well, at least that means Archie will go up into the sky like he's supposed to. But how are we going to find out what happened to him after he took off?

Missy picked off a few crumbs of stale bread and held them out towards Einstein. Einstein turned an even deeper shade of **green**. 'We all have to keep our strength up,' she said to him. 'Even if that means eating this rubbish.' Missy took a bite of the stale bread herself and gagged as she swallowed it. 'Did you see the scar on the guard's hand?' she whispered to Felix. 'I wonder if Aldini has one like that too?'

'That's *not* Aldini,' Felix whispered with certainty. 'If it was it would mean that he had a time machine too. How else would he be back here in 1943?'

Missy's brow creased as she thought this over. 'I suppose so,' she admitted.

'So we have to be back in the cell this afternoon when they come to march us off to see the colonel,' Bill said, washing down his bread with the murky water. 'That should be plenty of time for me to meet up with Stella, show her my plane and—'

'You're not leaving the cell,' Felix said, getting to his feet. 'Last night we were lucky they didn't catch us. What if they caught you escaping today? You're meant to be banged up in here with us, not swaggering around the base showing off to a girl. Not only would they think you're a spy, they'd think you were a deserter. You'd be executed for desertion! It's not worth the risk.'

Missy shot Felix a pleading look. He could tell what his friend was thinking, even without her saying anything. *If Bill is executed for treason then he'll never marry Stella, he'll never have kids or grandkids and she'll never be born!*

'Stella's worth the risk,' Bill said firmly. Missy couldn't help but smile as he said this. 'And I bet my bottom dollar that you two aren't planning to stay in the cell all day. Not with that nifty little hologram machine of yours.'

Felix stayed silent as he thought to himself. *Stay cooped up in this dingy prison all day? Is the Earth square? Of course not! We've got a job to do . . .*

'I didn't think so,' Bill said, seeing the look on Felix's face. 'However you plan to get out this time, you're taking me with you.'

'No, we're not,' Felix said sternly.

'Yes, we are,' Missy said, contradicting him.

For the love of Galileo! 'Missy! If Bill is caught and executed for desertion then . . .'

'That won't happen! We won't let it. He wants to see Stella!' She shrugged. 'Who are we to keep true love apart?'

Felix groaned. 'Fine, Bill, we'll take you with us on three conditions . . .'

'Anything,' Bill agreed quickly.

'Number one: you're back in the cell by the time they come to collect you. Number two: you do not – no matter what – fly your plane today.' *It needs to be Archie going up into the sky, not Bill.*

'And number three: you do whatever I tell you, whenever I tell you, without question. OK?'

'OK,' Bill said, excitement creeping on to his face at the thought of soon seeing Stella again. 'One question . . .'

Felix sighed. 'I said NO questions.'

'Just one.' Bill held up one finger. 'Before we get going?'

'Just one,' Felix agreed, taking the hologram box out of his bag and setting it up so images of the three of them were projected into the cell.

'I need to have a shower and comb my hair. Stella is the girl I'm going to marry – I'm sure of it. I don't want to go out there looking like something that's been spat out of a dusty engine. Will you help me do that? Will you?'

Felix let out an exasperated sigh.

Winking wormholes! When is this guy going to stop being as soppy as a supernova?

11
Up, Up and Away

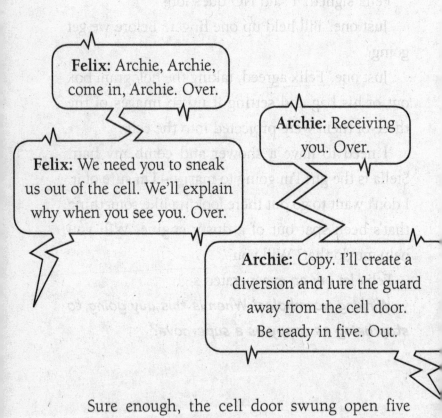

Felix: Archie, Archie, come in, Archie. Over.

Archie: Receiving you. Over.

Felix: We need you to sneak us out of the cell. We'll explain why when you see you. Over.

Archie: Copy. I'll create a diversion and lure the guard away from the cell door. Be ready in five. Out.

Sure enough, the cell door swung open five minutes later.

I never really saw the point in friends before, Felix thought to himself, seeing Archie at the cell door. *Science and maths were all I needed. But what Bill and Archie have is pretty special — Archie just came to Bill's rescue, no questions asked.* He looked over at Missy as she bent down and carefully picked Einstein off the cell floor and put him safely in her pocket. *I guess I'm lucky to have a friend like Missy too . . .*

With the hologram projecting the images of Felix, Missy and Bill into the cell, the three once again sneaked out into the corridor and the airbase beyond.

'Bill, you go with Archie,' Felix instructed. 'We'll meet up with you once we have Stella. Understand?'

Bill smiled back. 'Copy.'

While Bill and Archie disappeared towards the shower block, Felix and Missy crept around the airbase in the direction of the main gates.

Einstein poked his head out of Missy's pocket before scrambling down to the ground and running ahead. 'Good idea, buddy,' Felix whispered to his pet lizard. 'You can be a lookout.'

They ran towards a huge armoured vehicle that had a pair of mechanic's legs sticking out from beneath it. The doors to the driver's and passenger's seats were open and two men were sitting inside. Felix could hear their American accents chattering loudly as he and Missy crept towards them. He held his breath, trusting Einstein to alert them to danger as they approached. Without being spotted, Einstein led Felix and Missy around the large vehicle. His scales shone **purple**, giving them the all-clear, before he darted ahead and scuttled underneath a parked van. There was just enough room beneath the van for Felix and Missy to commando-crawl

after the lizard. They peeked out of the other side, watching the feet of airbase men walk past. Camouflaging himself into the gravelled ground, Einstein scampered ahead, and when the coast was clear he once again flashed them a bright **purple**.

Felix and Missy crawled out from beneath the van and darted across an open courtyard towards a parked car. The airbase's main gates were in sight. Felix and Missy quickly hid behind a bush so they could get a better look without being seen. Felix patted Einstein on the head in thanks, and his trusty pet smiled back at him.

'She's there!' Missy pointed towards Stella.

She was dressed in a pretty floral dress, her hair pinned into waves. She was standing at the guard hut by the main gates and speaking to a uniformed man. Stella was pointing inside the base and shrugging her shoulders.

'She probably thinks Bill stood her up,' Felix whispered to Missy. 'She's come all this way to see him and he's not here to meet her.'

'He can't just walk up to the main gates to meet her,' Missy said, flustered. 'He's meant to be in a cell! Oh this is bad, bad, bad. If they send Stella away, then she'll be so angry at Bill for standing her up she'll never want to see him again. Then they'll never get married and—'

Felix interrupted Missy before she could get too panicked: 'They won't let her into the base unless she has an official invite. Security's bound to be pretty tight. But I have an idea . . .'

Felix took his radio out of his pocket and began to twiddle the dial.

The radio crackled with static, every now and again hitting a dial tone or intercepting Morse code messages.

If I can just find the right frequency of the radio for the guard on the gate . . .

Suddenly the guard looked down at his radio and picked it up. **Bingo!**

With Stella and the guard in his sights, Felix pressed the walkie-talkie to his mouth and said . . .

Felix: This is the assistant to the colonel. Over.

Guard: Receiving. Over.

Felix: Orders are to let the lady at the gate into the base immediately. Over.

Guard: Really?

Felix: Are you questioning the colonel's orders?

Guard: No, sir. Of course not, sir.

Felix. Good. Let her in and say sorry for holding her up!

Felix held his breath in anticipation and he and Missy watched as the guard apologized profusely to Stella before waving her in to the base. Stella walked through the gates, looking around, not knowing where she was meant to be heading.

'Pst!' Missy called out to her. 'Over here!'

Stella looked towards the bush they were hiding behind, alarmed. 'Hello?'

'Over here.' Missy beckoned her.

Stella walked towards them.

'Behind the bush,' Missy directed her.

Stella peered behind the bush and Felix quickly pulled her towards them. The three of them stood, cramped and far too close for comfort.

'Um, hello.' Stella smiled, still looking confused. 'You're the girl from last night, aren't you?'

'Yes.' Missy shook her head, smiling. 'It's so nice to see you again.'

'It's nice to see you too,' Stella replied, slightly wary. 'But I'm supposed to be meeting Bill.'

'He's sent us to meet you and take you to him,' Felix said. 'We're your welcoming committee.'

Stella smiled. 'How sweet.'

'Bill's involved in top-secret work here at the airbase,' Missy added, trying to impress her. 'He couldn't tear himself away.'

'Although he's looking forward to seeing you,' Felix added. 'He's going to meet us by his plane.'

'I didn't realize that children worked here at Daws Hill,' Stella said, giving them a strange look. 'You two seem to know an awful lot about what's going on.'

'A lot of top-secret work goes on around here,' Missy said, straightening her shoulders and sounding confident. 'It's probably best for your own safety that you don't ask too many questions.'

'I see.' Stella blinked, startled by Missy's worldly tone.

Stella was too busy looking around at the planes, cars, tanks and military flags to notice the small lizard leading the way ahead of them through the base. Thanks to Einstein's signals, Felix and Missy were able to sneak Stella towards the planes without being noticed.

When they reached Archie and Bill, they found the friends standing by Bill's plane, deep in conversation.

Bill's hair had been washed and combed into his signature side parting. He smelt of soap and wore a freshly pressed uniform. Missy smiled at the sight of her great-grandfather looking so dashing.

'Stella!' Bill beamed as soon as he saw her.

'I was just telling Bill that I've been assigned to fly his plane this afternoon,' Archie told Felix and Missy, as Bill and Stella chatted away to each other. 'Since he's meant to be imprisoned,' Archie added quietly, so Stella couldn't hear, 'I've been tasked with taking this baby up into the skies and test-flying her ahead of a top-secret mission.' Archie patted the wing of the plane.

Phew! At least something's happening like it's supposed to. Now I just need to find a way to . . .

'I gotta say, buddy,' Bill said, holding Stella's hand and looking up at the plane, 'I'm kinda bummed that it's you flying her today and not me. But if it means I get to spend the day with Stella . . .' Stella beamed from ear to ear. 'So this is my plane,' Bill explained to Stella, pointing at the light bomber aircraft in front of them. 'Room for one pilot up front and a co-pilot in the back. When we're flying missions we sometimes fly solo so we can carry more fuel or cargo.'

'I've never flown in a plane before,' Stella said, looking up at the light aircraft in awe.

'I'll take you up,' Bill said quickly.

WHAT???

'What?' Missy said aloud.

'Come on,' Bill said persuasively. 'I'll do the test flight instead of Archie. Stella can come with me.'

Then they'll both disappear!

'Absolutely not,' Felix said, trying not to shout. 'You promised you wouldn't fly today. And you promised to do everything I asked you to do. Well, I'm asking you . . . no, I'm telling you – you cannot fly that plane.'

A man's voice boomed from behind them. 'Lieutenant Hudson!'

They spun around.

145

The colonel! Darwin's beard!

The colonel began to run towards them. 'Guards! Seize them!'

'What's going on?' asked Stella, seeing the look of panic on everyone's faces.

'No time to explain now,' Bill said.

Felix looked around. Guards had suddenly appeared out of nowhere and were running towards them from all angles. There was nowhere to hide. There was no way they were getting out of this one. And this time they were taking Stella and Archie with them!

'I'm innocent!' Bill screamed, holding Stella's hand tightly. 'I'm not a spy – none of us are! If you convict us and execute us for treason then you'll be making a terrible mistake.'

'Take aim – keep them in your sights. If they raise a weapon, don't hesitate to fire!' the colonel screamed at the guards. One by one they raised their rifles and took aim at the group in front of the plane.

'Only one option,' Archie shouted, backing towards the plane.

'The plane!' Bill screamed.

Before Felix could stop them, Archie had pulled down the steps to the aircraft and begun to climb. Bill helped Stella on to the first step. 'Time to take that flight you always wanted . . .'

'Wait!' Felix began to shout. But there was nothing else they could do.

'Felix, quick!' Missy climbed up the steps, and without thinking Felix followed her.

In a matter of seconds they were all crammed into the small cockpit.

There were only two seats – one for the pilot and

another behind for the co-pilot.

Bill and Stella shared the first seat, with Missy perched between their laps. Felix wedged himself in next to Archie at the back of the plane.

'Belts on, prepare for take-off!' Bill commanded from the front of the plane.

Felix grabbed on to the side of the cockpit as the plane began to move slowly down the runway.

The guards below started to shout and wave their fists, pulling back the triggers on their guns and aiming them at the aircraft.

'How will we take off?' Missy shouted, petrified. 'We're too heavy.'

'Drop a fuel tank,' Archie commanded Bill. 'And eject the bombs. We're too near the ground – they won't detonate. But we need to lose the weight, otherwise we'll never get off the ground.'

Bill flicked a bunch of switches and Felix felt the plane judder as it dropped the extra weight it was carrying.

Bill pulled back hard on the throttle and the plane sped down the runway with the force of a gale. The rush of the wind and the roar of the engine vibrated in Felix's ears. *This will deafen me!*

Before Felix could stop them they were leaning backward as the plane's nose lifted into the sky.

12
Nosedive

Well, fling me out to a far spiral of the galaxy and serve me a sundae! This could not have gone any more wrong if we'd been trying!

'Felix!' Missy shouted through the pilot's radio. Her voice boomed into the co-pilot's seat.

Felix picked up the co-pilot's radio next to him and shouted back, 'Missy!'

'This is bad,' Missy's voice crackled over the radio waves. 'This is so . . . so bad.'

She is not wrong!

The plane was flying as high as it could in the sky, considering it was carrying more weight than it was designed to.

'Felix, what can we do?' she screamed. 'Parachute

out of here?'

'There won't be enough chutes,' Felix yelled back. 'The plane's only meant to carry a crew of two!'

'Turn back and take our chances back on the airbase?'

'They'll shoot us out of the sky before we have a chance to land!'

The airbase, the angry colonel and guards below them were long gone. They were flying over small villages and green fields, and the shimmering blue of the sea was visible in the distance.

'We're heading towards the sea!' Missy screamed into the radio.

Felix heard Bill's voice behind her. 'I've got no choice. If I land the plane then we'll soon be rounded up and arrested.'

'Why are we running away?' Stella screamed. 'I don't understand!'

'The engine's going to blow out on us before we can land,' Archie said with concern. He was squished in beside Felix and frantically casting his eyes over the spinning dials on the plane's control panel. 'The wings' air flaps are showing signs of malfunction – if we'd had time to do the usual pre-flight checks before we took off then we might have detected a problem. Who knows – but if we don't fix them we'll be nosediving into the ocean before too long.'

'There must be something we can do,' Felix said.

'How much do you know about physics?' Archie asked, his brow pulling together tightly.

'More than any other twelve-year-old,' Felix answered honestly.

'I need someone to help me while Bill flies solo for a while.'

Felix nodded. 'OK.'

Archie took the plane's radio from Felix's hands and said to Bill, 'Me and Felix back here are going to try to pull out the wing flaps – help us get across this ocean.'

'We don't have enough fuel,' Bill radioed back urgently. 'There's no way we'll make it. We're all—'

'Just let us try,' Archie pleaded with Bill.

'I can hold her for two minutes,' Bill said, as Archie unstrapped himself from the seat and put his co-pilot controls on autopilot. 'Then I need your help again.'

In the name of Newton . . . !

To Felix's horror, he watched as Archie began to reach for the lock on the roof to the co-pilot's seat.

'There's too much wind-pressure,' Felix warned him. 'If you open the roof the force of the wind will suck us out of the plane and throw us towards the ground!'

'Take this!' Archie threw Felix a harness that was attached to an extendable wire. 'Put it on,' he instructed, as he put on a harness of his own. 'We need to climb out of the cockpit and on to the wing. This will stop us falling down to earth if we slip.'

Felix felt his heart lurch like a tidal wave inside him.

Climb out of the cockpit?! On to the wing, while the plane is flying?! Has this guy completely lost his mind?!

'Put it on!' Archie screamed at Felix.

Felix fumbled with the harness until it was sitting tight around his chest.

What am I doing? How has this happened? I want to go home!

'You're too young to know about Newton's third law of motion,' Archie said, once again reaching for the lock on the cockpit roof, 'but when you apply it to the flight of a plane . . .'

'Air gives the plane an upward force,' Felix said quickly. *As if I don't understand Newton's third law of motion!* 'So the plane must give an equal and opposite downward force to the air. The plane generates lift by using the wings to push down air behind it.'

'Exactly,' Archie said. He looked impressed.

'That's why a plane's wings aren't flat – so they can direct airflow downward to make the plane lift into the sky,' Felix added.

'So I guess you already know that a plane has special flaps on its wings that can extend to push more air down?'

Felix nodded. 'They're used at take-off and landing.'

'Well, we also need to use those flaps now,' Archie said, unlocking the roof. 'But the engine's not letting us, which only leaves us one option . . .'

The roof to the cockpit flew open and Felix felt himself being pulled upward by the force of the moving plane. He grabbed hold of the side of the cockpit and watched in horror as Archie climbed out of the cockpit and began to crawl towards the wing.

He wants us to pull up the air flaps so the plane stays in the air! This is insane! It'll never work!

Felix felt Einstein leap from his pocket. He watched as the lizard scuttled to safety in the footwell of the plane, his scales glowing a frightening shade of **red**. *I don't blame him,* Felix thought. *I'd hide away if I could. But I can't. This plane cannot nosedive into the ocean; we need to do what we can to keep it in flight!*

Before Felix could stop himself, he was clambering out of the plane and on to the wing.

Great Galileo!

The force of the wind rushing by made the skin on his face ripple like a wave, and he couldn't hear a thing. Every part of him shook as he willed his numb hands to pull him further up the wing.

The plane tilted in the sky, dropping the wing that Felix clung to lower than the one that Archie was on. Felix had a clear view of Archie: he was already lying flat on the other wing. He was trying to pull out the jammed wing flaps, but having no luck.

Felix wriggled his body over the wing, his limbs rigid with fear.

He reached the first wing flap and dug his fingers around it, trying with all his strength to pull it out.

My backpack! He looked back towards the cockpit of the plane. At the front were Bill, Stella and Missy – Missy was screaming at him but he couldn't hear what she was saying over the sound of the wind. And behind them, in the co-pilot's seat, was Felix's backpack. *My aviation toolkit! If I could just reach it . . .*

The plane lurched downward and Felix felt the contents of his stomach do somersaults inside him. He gripped on to the plane for everything his life was worth.

There was no way he could make it back to the cockpit. There was no way he could do anything but cling on to the wing for dear life – if he moved a muscle he'd be dead.

I have the harness to save me . . . . maybe I could . . .

The plane lurched downward once again.

They were dangerously close to the water now.

Felix felt the ocean spray begin to tickle his face from the crashing waves below.

We're going down! he realized in horror. *We're going to hit the water. There's nothing we can do. This is how I die, right here and now on the wing of a light bomber in 1943 . . .*

That was the last thought Felix had before the plane nosedived towards the churning water.

13
Secret Submarine

'Back home in Virginia, and during the war, in the First Eight, I was one of the best pilots around . . .' Felix remembered Bill's words as the water zoomed towards them. *Come on, Bill,* he willed. *You can do it. If anyone can land a plane on water, it's you . . .*

Just as the plane was about to pierce the water, Bill managed to do the impossible . . .

The plane skimmed the water's surface, slowing to a halt and then bobbing on top of the waves.

'You did it!' Missy screamed from the front of the plane. The top hatch of the pilot's seat flew open. Missy's head poked out of the top and she looked around at the endless ocean surrounding them in awe. 'You landed the plane on water!'

'Planes can float on water?' Stella said, amazed.

'It won't float forever,' Felix shouted towards them, still lying on the wing and gripping hard on to one of the air flaps. 'Turn the engine off,' he shouted over at Bill. 'Otherwise the engine will suck up water and flip the plane over.'

And even if we don't flip, Felix thought to himself, *we have twenty minutes MAX before the plane takes in too much water and sinks.* He looked around, desperate to see any kind of land. There was nothing. *Great guzzling geysers . . .*

'Is there a life raft on board?' Felix shouted, already knowing the answer would be a big fat no. 'Life jackets? Rubber rings?' *The plane didn't take extra fuel on a flight because of the weight — why would it have a life raft?*

'No,' said Archie, now standing up on the other wing and trying to find his balance. He looked ridiculous. *Like he's going surfing on the wing of a plane!* 'We couldn't afford the extra weight,' he confirmed.

Missy caught Felix's eye. She must have been able to tell what he was thinking. 'The plane's going to sink soon, isn't it?'

Felix nodded, worried. 'Can everyone swim?' he asked.

'I can't,' Stella said, poking her head out of the pilot's seat and looking worried.

'OK, don't panic,' Felix said, finally finding the

160

strength and balance to pull himself to sitting on the wing of the floating plane. 'I'll think of something. We just need to . . .'

Suddenly the waves around them began to part, as though a huge whale was about to rear its head from the water. The plane wobbled from side to side, and both Archie and Felix were knocked flat on their backs on the wings.

But it wasn't a whale that rose out of the water.

It was a runway.

Did I hit my head when the plane crash-landed? Felix looked around him in disbelief. Rising out of the water, as clear as the sun in the sky, was a short runway. *This cannot be happening . . .*

'Felix, look!' Missy shouted, pointing to something behind them. Felix looked back to see a submarine rising out of the water. The runway was attached to the submarine, and was extending out on to the surface of the ocean, like a huge retractable arm.

'A submarine!' Bill stood up in the cockpit and pointed at the metal beast rising out of the water. 'It's come to rescue us. But what kind of submarine has an extendable runway?'

A state-of-the-art military submarine, Felix realized. *A submarine that belongs to someone very, very important . . .*

The sound of the water crashing around them filled Felix's ears as the submarine moved so the runway was now sitting directly beneath their plane.

At least now we won't sink!

'Bill!' Archie shouted, once again standing up on the wing. 'Buddy, you got your gun handy?'

'Sure do,' Bill shouted back.

'Why do you need guns?' Missy said, alarmed. 'These people have come to save us.'

'For all we know this could be an enemy sub – a Nazi U-boat,' Bill shouted, taking up his rifle. 'They could have come to capture us. We don't know.'

Felix took a deep breath as he remembered everything he'd ever read about Nazi U-boats in World War Two . . .

Nazi U-boats:

* Nazi U-boats were the largest fleet of submarines in World War Two.

* The enemy used U-boats to devastating effect – taking out British merchant ships and destroying food and military supplies that were urgently needed.

* U-boats would hunt Allied boats in 'wolf packs'.

* Their main weapon was torpedoes. They also used mines and guns.

* By the end of the war nearly 3,000 Allied ships had been sunk by U-boats, and thousands of brave souls had lost their lives.

If this really is a Nazi U-boat, then we are all doomed. *How has this situation just gone from bad to worse . . . ?*

Felix bit down on his lip, tasting the salt of seawater spray, and watched with bated breath as a hatch on the side of the submarine opened up.

They waited in silence for someone to appear from within the submarine. *Will they be wearing enemy uniform, or will they be one of us?* In the split second of stillness, Felix tried to recall the Nazi navy uniforms . . . *A white-and-blue shirt with three stripes on the collar, a cap with two ribbons on it, a silk neckerchief . . .*

They waited and waited. But no one came.

After a few long minutes it was obvious that no one was coming out.

'They want us to go in,' Missy said, the hope clear in her voice.

'We can't go in there,' Bill said quickly. 'If it is the enemy then we'll be walking straight into a trap.'

'What choice do we have?' Felix pointed out, feeling frustrated. 'A few minutes ago we were all about to sink into the ocean. This is our only chance of survival. We have to take it.'

'He's right,' Archie said, nodding, not taking his eyes from the submarine hatch. 'Let's go.'

Very slowly Bill helped Missy and Stella climb out of the cockpit and on to the runway that was now sitting beneath them. The runway was still barely above the water's surface, and water sloshed over their feet as they jumped down on to it.

Felix led the way, with Archie and the others behind him. As he walked along the extendable runway to the submarine's hatch, he saw a bright red object dart ahead of him. 'Einstein!' he said quickly. 'It's too dangerous for you to go alone as lookout. Come on to my shoulder, we'll go in together.' Einstein stopped running and looked back at Felix. His scales turned a shade of **purple** for yes, and as Felix came near to him he leaped up and sat bravely on Felix's shoulder.

Together, Felix and Einstein approached the open hatch. Felix put one foot over the threshold and took a deep breath.

'Be careful, Felix,' he heard Missy say behind him.

One small step for man, one giant leap for Felix Frost . . .

The first thing he saw inside the hatch was a ladder. Without a second thought he began to climb down.

As his feet finally touched the floor he turned around . . .

He was in the middle of the submarine control room. There were computer screens, control panels and high-tech navigation systems all around him.

This. Is. Incredible.

The light inside the control room was dim and reddish.

Ahead of him were four computer screens. Felix approached, his mouth hanging open.

On the first computer screen was a pixellated image of their plane sitting on the runway. On the second and third were images of the water surrounding them. And on the fourth computer screen were the words:

COME IN

'What does it say?' Missy asked, now standing behind Felix.

Felix looked back, and saw that Archie, Bill and Stella had followed him into the control room, their eyes wide and their mouths agape.

Felix turned back and pointed to the screen. 'They want us to go in.'

'Through there.' Missy pointed to a dark corridor ahead of them.

As Felix headed towards it, he tried to remember everything he'd ever read about World War Two submarines . . .

* The Jolly Roger is the emblem of the Royal Navy Submarine Service.

* To work on a submarine you must complete the notorious 'Perisher' training – one of the toughest military courses in the world!

* One of the most famous Royal Navy submarines in World War Two was HMS Upholder, which went missing in 1942. No ship debris or bodies were ever found, but it's assumed that it was sunk and all aboard died.

* Seventy-four British submarines were lost during World War Two.

At the end of the corridor was a small room. Three men stood there. Two men were in Royal Navy uniforms, and the man standing in the middle was wearing a suit. Felix recognized him instantly.

'Winston Churchill!'

'Welcome to HMS *Chartwell*. Now explain to me please,' said Winston Churchill – he was wearing a fine suit with a black bow tie – 'why two American pilots, a female civilian and two children have crash-landed a light bomber plane over the North Sea?'

'I can explain, Mr Churchill,' Missy said, pushing herself in front of Felix.

Here we go . . .

'We had to escape a mad colonel back at RAF Daws Hill,' she said quickly. Churchill watched her in amazement, his lip twitching into what looked like a smile. 'These two men –' she pointed back to Archie and Bill – 'are two of the finest pilots in the First Eight.'

'They're involved in Operation Chastise,' Felix blurted out. 'They're that good.'

Churchill's face suddenly went an alarming shade of pink. 'What do you know about Operation

Chastise? It's a top-secret operation and . . . is that a lizard on your shoulder?'

'Yes,' Felix said proudly. 'This is Einstein.'

'Einstein?' Churchill spluttered in astonishment. 'The mad scientist from Germany?! What does a child know about Albert Einstein?'

'Albert Einstein isn't a mad scientist!' Felix corrected Churchill. 'He developed the general theory of relativity. And . . . ouch!'

Missy punched Felix hard in the shoulder.

'You're right, Mr Churchill. Most children alive now don't know anything about Albert Einstein.' She cast Felix a filthy look. 'But . . . we . . . we're not normal children.'

Churchill cocked an eyebrow. 'That much is obvious.'

'And we're NOT spies,' Felix added quickly.

Missy shrugged. 'We just want to help.'

'We want to serve our countries,' Bill added, stepping forward.

'And defeat the enemy,' Archie said with passion.

'We'll do anything we can to help,' Stella pleaded.

Winston Churchill cast his eyes up and down

the line of unlikely heroes who stood before him. If anyone was going to help him win World War Two it wasn't likely to be two bedraggled American pilots, a civilian woman and two children – one with a lizard on his shoulder!

'I know it seems utterly bonkers,' Churchill mumbled. 'But there's something I like about you lot. You can stay on the submarine overnight. But first thing tomorrow you must fly back to your base and explain yourself to this "mad" colonel you were so desperate to get away from.'

Felix looked around the small room. The walls were pinned with scraps of paper with equations and codes scrawled across them.

Codes to break? One of my favourite things!

'Thank you, Mr Churchill.' Felix smiled, and pointed at a code pinned up on the wall. 'And I think I'll be able to help you out with some of these . . .'

14
The Dream Team

Codebreaking – the facts:

✳ The Spartans are credited with creating the first system of secret codes. This is why the study of secret codes is called cryptology, from the Greek word kryptos meaning 'secret'.

✳ Codebreakers are known as cryptanalysts.

✳ Military strategies and secret battle plans were communicated by complex codes during World War Two.

✳ Advanced mathematics was used to decipher enemy codes.

✳ The enemy used Enigma machines to scramble Morse code messages.

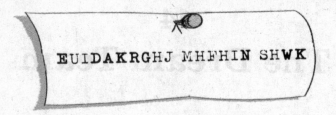

EUIDAKRGHJ MHFHIN SHWK

Felix had been staring at the jumble of letters on a scrap of paper pinned to the wall for over an hour.

The Navy commanders aboard the submarine with Churchill had taken one look at Felix, Missy, Bill, Stella and Archie and decided that after landing a plane on water they were in need of a good meal.

The first thing they had done after Churchill had agreed they could stay on HMS *Chartwell* overnight was scoff down a full dinner of tinned corned beef, tinned cabbage and tinned plum pudding.

Felix had never liked corned beef, cabbage or plum pudding. But that evening, on a submarine somewhere off the coast of England, he'd never tasted anything better.

After the large meal Missy, Bill and Stella had sat themselves down in a corner. Bill and Stella were chatting away, getting to know each other, and Missy was listening in with a contented smile on her face.

Jeez, Missy! Now is not the time for romance! Felix had thought to himself. *Now is the time for codebreaking!*

Archie obviously felt the same way as Felix did. Because as soon as they'd eaten, both Felix and Archie headed straight off to study the enemy codes pinned up on the walls of the submarine.

Among the many codes and charts on the wall was one large code printed out. A few pieces of paper with failed attempts to crack the code were pinned next to it.

'This one is most urgent,' Churchill said, pointing to the code.

Felix stared at it again.

EUIDAKRGHJ MHFHIN SHWK

'It looks like it should be a keyword cipher,' Felix said thoughtfully, staring at the letters.

'What's that?' Archie asked.

'It's when a secret-code keyword is placed at the beginning of the alphabet, and that shifts the remaining letters of the alphabet, not used in the keyword, to the right.'

'I see,' said Archie, understanding straight away. 'So you use the keyword alphabet to write the secret message, instead of the normal alphabet.'

'It seems you two have a natural flare for codebreaking,' Winston Churchill said, smiling. 'If you manage to crack this, I'll be in your debt. We think this is a message about an imminent enemy attack. We need to know when and where the attack will take place or hundreds, maybe thousands, of people may die.'

'Leave it with us,' Archie said and smiled.

Churchill began to walk away.

'Before you go,' Felix said quickly, 'can you tell us anything about how the message was intercepted? It might help us crack the keyword cipher.'

'We've intercepted a few messages from this station

before,' Churchill said thoughtfully. 'They're being broadcast from a military base that was used as an English-speaking university before the war. The soldiers coding the messages must know quite a bit about science as some of the keywords we've cracked have been English and scientific in nature . . . atom, quark, uranium, mechanics . . .'

Felix smiled. **Perfect**, he thought. 'Thank you, Mr Churchill, we'll do our best.'

'Good luck,' Churchill said, adding, 'you'll need it – this code is proving impossible to crack.'

Churchill left Felix, Einstein and Archie staring at the wall where the intercepted code had been pinned up. Felix mulled over the letters, already running through ideas in his head of what the keyword to crack the code might be.

Archie chewed his lip, his brow pulling together in thought. 'The code's keyword could be another scientific word?' he suggested to Felix. 'Particle? Orbit? Gravity? Nuclear?'

Felix stared at the paper, his eyes unblinking. 'Good ideas. But none of those work,' he said with certainty.

'Back when me and Bill were kids we used to write little codes to one another,' Archie said, not taking his eyes off the code on the wall. 'Nothing as sophisticated as this,' he said, pointing to the code in front of them. 'Always thought I was pretty good at it – but this is a toughie!'

'Did you ever consider becoming a codebreaker, instead of a pilot?' Felix asked Archie, still staring ahead at the code.

'Of course!' Archie's eyes lit up. 'Flying planes was my first love but maths and codebreaking always came a close second.'

'Maybe once the war is over . . .'

'I'll hang up my flight suit and become a mathematician,' Archie said. 'Who knows what will happen after the war? Who knows if the war will ever end? Who will win? What will the world look like in the future if the Nazis take over?'

Felix bit down on his lip. *I wish I could tell him that it's all going to be OK. That we'll win the war and the world will be a better place. But if Archie knew I was a time travelling whizz-kid*

his brain might just explode all over this coded
message — then we'll never solve it!

'Hey,' Archie said excitedly. 'Maybe the keyword's not just a word — maybe it's a name. A famous scientist.'

Felix's eyes lit up. 'You ARE good at this, Archie. That's an awesome idea. Einstein, Strassmann, Bohr . . .'

'Newton? Galileo? Copernicus?' Archie said, never looking away from the code on the paper.

'They don't work,' Felix said, quickly trying them out as keywords in his head. 'Besides, I have a hunch that it's a more modern name; a scientist alive now in 1943. Someone like . . . I've got it!'

Felix grabbed a pencil and a scrap of blank paper. He wrote out the alphabet on one line and on the line below it he wrote the word 'Heisenberg' followed by the rest of the alphabet, leaving out the letters already used in 'Heisenberg'.

ABCDEFGHIJKLMNOPQRSTUVWXYZ
HEISNBRGACDFJKLMOPQTUVWXYZ

'Who . . . what is Heisenberg?' Archie asked, bemused.

'He's a German physicist,' Felix said, excited, sure that he was close to cracking the code. 'Born in 1901, he's one of the pioneers of quantum mechanics. He won the Nobel Prize for Physics in 1932 for his paper laying out the neutron-proton model of the nucleus.'

'OK,' Archie replied, clearly not having a clue what Felix was on about. 'But does it work? Does Heisenberg's name work as the keyword cipher?'

Felix used the chart he'd written out to unscramble the coded message.

EUIDAKRGHJ MHFHIN SHWK =
BUCKINGHAM PALACE DAWN

'The enemy are planning an attack on Buckingham Palace at dawn!' Felix screamed at the top of his lungs.

At the sound of Felix's yell, Missy, Bill and Stella came rushing over, concern etched on their faces.

Churchill and his military advisers were close behind them.

'Let me see that.' Churchill snatched the decoded message clean out of Felix's hands. His eyes roved over the message. 'You've done it! You've cracked the code!' His face lit up with joy. He turned to his military advisers. 'Get on the radio – communicate with HQ back in London that a dawn attack on Buckingham Palace is imminent. Evacuate the palace – get the king, the queen and the princesses to safety – and tell the anti-aircraft guns to stand by.'

Once his advisers had hurried away to obey his command, Churchill turned to face Felix and Archie. 'You two are heroes. The work you have done here this evening will not only have saved the lives of the royal family, but the hundreds of people who work at Buckingham Palace every day. You obviously have a natural talent for codebreaking.'

'It was all Felix's work,' Archie admitted.

'You helped too,' Felix said, reassuring him.

'I could use talent like yours here. I'd like to offer you both a position here with me on HMS *Chartwell*. If you agree, then your job will be to remain here and work with the Allies' top military leaders to crack enemy codes and save more lives.'

'I accept,' Archie said without hesitation.

Hmm, thought Felix. *Life as a codebreaker in World War Two . . . tempting. But that's not why I came back here.*

'I'm honoured,' Felix said to Churchill. 'But I can't stay here. If I'm not back home to do my chores by dinnertime then my mum will have my head on a platter!'

Churchill smiled. 'I understand. But when

you're older I hope very much that you will serve your country using that amazing brain of yours.' Felix smiled. 'And as for you –' Churchill spoke to Archie – 'welcome aboard!' Archie beamed with pride. 'Now that you are a member of our secret team you'll be required to leave your previous life behind. You must commit yourself one hundred per cent to this calling. Once you join the secret service I'm afraid you can never go back to normal life. To the rest of the world it will simply seem as though you have completely disappeared.'

'But what about the mission?' Bill said to his best friend. 'What about flying planes and helping the First Eight to win the war? What about your family?'

'They have you for that,' Archie said to Bill.

'You're the best pilot they have. My place is here now. This is where I want to be. My family would understand.'

'So you're just going to disappear, without a word?' Bill said, alarmed.

'You'll hear from me again,' Archie reassured him. 'I promise.'

Churchill clapped his hands together! 'That's settled then! Archie will stay here with us on HMS *Chartwell* and help win the war from beneath the sea. Bill will return to RAF Daws Hill with this lovely lady here –' he smiled at Stella and she blushed – 'and help win the war from the skies. And you two –' he looked at Felix and Missy, then Einstein – 'and you . . . you will make sure you're home in time for dinner.'

'There's only one problem,' Bill said. 'The colonel thinks we're spies. We had to escape in the plane so his guards didn't shoot us.'

Churchill nodded. 'Leave the colonel to me. I know just what to do . . .'

MAY 14 1943

PM 2200

AIR 15/161/020

FELIX FROST, MISSY SIX, BILL
HUDSON AND STELLA FORD ARE TO
BE WELCOMED BACK TO RAF DAWS
HILL WITH OPEN ARMS STOP THEY
HAVE BEEN WORKING WITH ME ON
A TOP-SECRET MISSION TO CRACK
ENEMY CODES AND SAVE LIVES STOP
THEY ARE NOT TO BE PUNISHED FOR
ANYTHING THEY HAVE DONE STOP
INCLUDING STEALING A PLANE STOP
THEY ARE NOT SPIES STOP REPEAT
STOP NOT SPIES STOP THEY ARE TO BE
TREATED AS HEROES STOP THE DREAM
TEAM STOP

THIS IS A DIRECT ORDER.

WINSTON CHURCHILL

15
Homemade Parachutes

'The difference between a seaplane and a normal aeroplane —' Felix explained to Missy as he neatly placed the tools in his homemade aviation kit back into his backpack — 'is that a seaplane can land and take off on water as well as dry land.'

Missy nodded, looking at Bill's plane sat on HMS *Chartwell*'s sea runway in front of them. 'So it's like an amphibian. Like a toad, or a newt.'

Felix scratched his head. 'Good analogy. I never thought of it that way before.'

That's one thing I really like about Missy, Felix thought, looking over at his friend. *She gets it. She gets me. It feels nice to have someone understand me. I'm not about to tell her that though! Haloes and galaxies, she'd never let me hear the end of it!*

After only a few hours' sleep the night before, Felix had woken Missy and led her through the top-secret military submarine, up the ladder and out of the hatch so that they could repair the damage sustained to the aeroplane when it had nosedived towards the ocean.

Not only had Felix tinkered with the clapped-out engine and fixed the busted wing flaps, he'd also made a few simple modifications to the plane to help them fly back to base.

'Now the plane can take off on water as well as land,' Felix said proudly, looking over the aircraft and the changes he had made. 'Now there's just one more thing to do . . .'

With great care, Felix scratched his initials into the side of the plane using his penknife. Felix had been carving his signature into his inventions ever since he could remember. 'ᚠᚠ' had been carved on to the side of his cotton fuser, his rocket launcher and even his time machine.

'But we're standing on a runway,' Missy pointed out, as Felix stood back to once again admire his handiwork. 'Can't we just take off on that?'

'By my calculations the runway won't be long enough,' Felix explained. 'The weight of the plane – even without Archie on it – and the drag needed to lift the plane into the air . . .'

Missy frowned. 'Skip the technical parts, Felix.'

'The plane will need to move over the water before it lifts off,' Felix said with certainty. 'That's why we've fixed these on to the wings.' He pointed to the old plastic water butts that he and Missy had

attached to the wings. 'They'll help the plane float on water for the time it needs to gather more speed and take off into the air.'

'So we take off into the air,' said Missy. 'What then? What about the story of the ghost plane? We can't just land the plane back at the base and erase that story from history.'

'No,' agreed Felix. 'We can't. Don't worry, I have a plan. It involves parachutes . . .'

'Parachutes?' questioned Missy. 'But there are no parachutes on the plane – the plane couldn't take the extra weight.'

Felix shrugged. 'Not a problem. We'll just make parachutes.'

'MAKE parachutes?' Missy nearly fell over with shock. 'Are you insane?! Actually, don't answer that . . . you obviously are if you think I'm going to jump out of a plane with a homemade parachute!'

'You travelled back to 1943 with a homemade time machine,' Felix pointed out. 'And lived to tell the tale so far. You trust me, don't you?'

As if I could build a time machine and not a parachute!

Missy stared at Felix for a few long hard moments. She chewed down on her bottom lip and weighed up the dangers of trusting Felix to make a parachute that worked.

'I suppose you're right,' she said eventually. 'If I'm crazy enough to travel back in time with you, then I'm crazy enough to jump out of a plane with you.'

Felix beamed in triumph.

'How exactly do you plan to make a parachute?'

'Easy!' Felix smiled. 'A parachute needs to be made out of light, strong cloth,' he explained.

'Where are we going to find light, strong cloth in the middle of the ocean?'

'Come with me . . .' Felix led the way back into the submarine. They climbed down the ladder and made their way through the warren of dark submarine rooms until they arrived at a door that had a large sign pinned to the front.

WINSTON CHURCHILL
KEEP OUT

'Felix!' Missy whispered through gritted teeth. 'We can't just . . .'

Felix pushed open the door and walked right into the room.

He flicked on the light switch and marched over to the bed.

Missy shyly tiptoed into the room and looked around in awe. 'This must be Winston Churchill's top-secret submarine bedroom.' The walls were covered with family photos and spread out over a large oak desk in the corner of the room was a creased naval map with small model boats and submarines dotted all over the ocean. 'This must be where he's doing top-secret military planning. Felix, what are you . . . ?'

Felix ripped back the sheets from Churchill's bed and smiled. 'Just as I suspected – silk!'

'Silk sheets?' Missy looked confused.

'Light and strong – perfect parachute material!'

Missy helped Felix strip the bed. He took his toolkit from his bag and began instructing Missy. 'Cut down this line here,' he said, pointing. 'Now we need to sew this edge to this edge . . . and here . . .' He passed her some super-strength rope from his bag. 'Unravel some of the rope, thin it out and sew it into the sheet like this . . .'

Working as a team, Felix and Missy tore and patched up the silk sheets and sewed in super-strength rope. In no time at all they had created two large super-strong parachutes.

Suddenly the door swung open and Winston Churchill walked into the room.

He took one look at the two friends ripping up his expensive silk sheets. 'What the devil . . . ?!'

'It's for the war effort,' Felix explained. 'We had to make parachutes.'

Churchill frowned. 'You could have asked first, but –' he paused for thought and smiled – 'I admire your bravery and initiative – you remind me of myself when I was young.'

Wow, what a compliment!

'Your friends are ready to go,' Churchill said, holding the door open for Felix and Missy.

They walked back through the submarine and up, out on to the sea runway.

Bill and Stella were standing hand in hand, as Bill was deep in conversation with Archie.

'What should I tell everyone?' Bill said to Archie, a sad look on his face.

'You'll think of something,' Archie replied. 'And don't feel bad about lying. Whatever you do you can't let anyone know about HMS *Chartwell*. Don't ever let anyone know that I stayed here to help Churchill. My duty – my life – is here now. This is where I'm needed. It's where I want to be.'

Bill nodded, tears in the corners of his eyes. 'You've always been my best friend, buddy. I can't imagine not seeing you again.'

'I'll find a way to contact you,' Archie said quickly. 'I promise. Every year, on your birthday I'll send you a card. I won't write on it – I won't risk anyone knowing it's me. But you'll know that it was me who sent it.'

'How?' Bill asked.

'You just will.' Archie smiled.

The two friends hugged goodbye, then Archie turned and gave Stella a long hug too. 'Take care of him for me,' he whispered to her.

'I will,' Stella promised with a smile.

Churchill stood and watched as Bill, Stella, Missy and Felix climbed into the plane that they'd crash-landed on the ocean only a day before.

'I'd better go here this time,' Felix said, climbing into the pilot's cockpit at the front of the plane. Missy squeezed herself in beside him, and Bill and Stella crammed themselves into the co-pilot's seat at the back of the plane. 'It's going to be a bumpy ride,' Felix warned. 'And here –' he passed one of the parachutes to Bill – 'strap this on, and strap Stella to you. When I give the order we need to jump from the plane. We only had enough material for two parachutes so we're jumping in tandem. Missy, you're with me . . .'

Missy took a deep breath, strapping herself to Felix and the parachute. 'OK.'

'Fly well!' Churchill shouted, as Felix revved up the plane's engine. 'You're always welcome back here, Felix Frost. And I meant what I said last night – one day I hope you use that first-class brain of yours to serve your country.'

Felix gave Winston Churchill his best salute.

'You're doing an incredible job, sir. In my opinion Hitler and the Nazis aren't gonna last much longer.'

Missy elbowed him in the ribs. 'Felix! Don't say too much!'

Felix looked at the endless stretch of ocean ahead of them. He pressed down on the accelerator and prepared for lift-off. 'Hold tight, guys. Oh, and we're taking a detour before we go back to base.' Missy raised an eyebrow at him. He smiled at her and began to run the plane down the runway. 'Let's see what World War Two London looks like from the skies . . .'

16
The Blitz

Felix pumped the plane's engine into full throttle and began to speed it down the runway. Soon the runway had ended and the plane was gliding on water.

Felix's modifications worked perfectly, and the plane skimmed the top of the ocean with ease.

Woo-hoo! Shooting stars and asteroids! I should have made my own seaplane years ago. This is wicked fun!

The plane's nose lifted up into the air and everyone on board gripped their seats with white knuckles as they rose into the sky.

Once they were flying high above the ocean, they looked down and could just make out Churchill and

Archie still waving up at them from HMS *Chartwell*.
Soon the small figures were no larger than specks on
the horizon, and then they disappeared from sight
completely. Only miles and miles of endless blue
ocean stretched out in every
direction around them.

Felix felt little claws dig into his thigh as Einstein
clung on to him inside his trouser pocket. 'It's OK,
buddy,' Felix said to the small lizard. 'You stay
tucked away in there until we're safe on dry land.'

'Felix,' Missy said suddenly beside him. 'How do you even know how to fly a plane?'

Felix shrugged. 'I've read a few books on aviation skills. And when I was eight I invented my own flight simulator. It was awesome. I used to come back from school and sit in it for hours. I built the control pad in the cockpit to resemble a modern-day Boeing – so a bit different from this – but the principles of flight are roughly the same.'

'What happened to it?' Missy asked. 'I don't remember seeing it in your room.'

'It's not there any more,' Felix replied, not taking his eyes from the ocean ahead. 'I broke it down and used the parts for other inventions. Some of the wires and the fuse board even made it into the time machine.'

'Felix.' Bill's voice came over the radio from the cockpit behind. 'Shouldn't we be turning left to head for RAF Daws Hill?'

'We're flying back over London,' Felix replied over the radio.

Felix flew the plane skillfully back over the ocean, and dry land was soon visible on the

199

horizon. The clouds parted as the plane glided effortlessly through the skies. The plane soared over huge white cliffs, over meadows and fields, the grass and flowers swaying in the breeze. Small towns and villages dotted the landscape, and farms, churches, fields and rivers slipped away below them as they flew.

'Felix, look.' Missy was pointing to a huge crater in a field.

It looks like an asteroid has crash-landed!

'It must have been a bomb,' Missy said sadly, shaking her head. 'The Nazis must have dropped it from one of their planes.'

'Well, at least it landed in a field and not on a . . .' Felix didn't finish what he was about to say. Ahead of them was a large pile of bricks surrounding another huge crater in the earth. Bricks, rubble, books, clothes and broken furniture were strewn all over the surrounding fields. It was obvious what had happened. A bomb had hit a house.

Felix felt his stomach sink heavily inside him. He knew the facts about the Blitz, how thousands of people had lost their lives in the heavy bombing in World War Two. But seeing the destruction and devastation for himself was so much worse than any grim statistic he had ever read in a history book. Felix felt his eyes sting and prickle.

Evidence of bomb attacks became more frequent. Houses, villages, farms and even what looked like a school had been flattened by falling bombs. The devastation became worse as the houses and villages grew closer together.

'These bombs must have been dropped early,' Missy whispered in horror. 'Before the Nazi planes even reached London.'

'If the lights of London are out during a blackout,' Bill explained, 'then the Nazi planes can't see what they're bombing – sometimes they hit their intended targets, sometimes they don't.'

Soon the sprawling metropolis of London city was stretching out beneath the plane. The grey- and red-bricked buildings below them looked like toy houses, and the small roads and alleyways snaked towards a large blue river that ran like a vein throughout the city.

The River Thames.

Felix followed the Thames. Below he could see landmarks he recognized from modern-day London. Big Ben and the Houses of Parliament, St Paul's Cathedral, Tower Bridge, and even Buckingham Palace. *At least that's one place we managed to save,* Felix thought, looking down on the palace. *Everyone inside would have been killed if it had been bombed by the Nazis. But we stopped it. We broke the Nazis' secret code and foiled their plans.*

Felix allowed himself a little smile. *It feels good to know that we've done something to help.*

But Felix's smile soon faded as he once again looked at the passing scenes below. Entire streets had been flattened by Nazi bombs. Houses, hospitals, churches and parks had been destroyed by the war on the home front.

The facts are horrendous, Felix thought sadly, as he tried to concentrate on flying and not what he was seeing below.

The Blitz – the facts:

* The word 'Blitz' comes from the German word blitzkrieg, meaning 'lightning war'.

* 'The Blitz' was the name given to the period in World War Two when enemy bombs fell on London and other cities in England.

* The attack on London by Nazi bombers started on 7 September 1940, and it didn't end until May 1941.

* Sirens would warn people when enemy planes were approaching.

* People built their own air-raid shelters to hide from the bombs. They also used to hide below ground in places like underground Tube stations.

* At one point during the Blitz, London was bombed for fifty-seven nights in a row.

* During the Blitz over 32,000 British civilians were killed and 87,000 were seriously injured. Countless family pets were also killed and over two million homes were completely destroyed.

At least they had air-raid shelters and old Tube stations to hide away from the bombs in, Felix thought. *No wonder Gaga Bill doesn't like talking about the war. And no wonder he wishes that we never have to live through anything so dreadful.* Felix glanced over at Missy. She was staring out of the window, lost in her own sad thoughts. *I guess we're very lucky to be born at a time when things like this aren't happening to us.*

Soon the city of London and the evidence of heavy enemy bombing began to thin out. Soon, on the horizon, Felix could just about make out the shape of RAF Daws Hill.

'That's it!' Missy pointed into the distance. 'That's the airbase.'

Felix nodded. 'Time to put this bad boy on autopilot . . .'

He fiddled with the aeroplane's computer, flicked switches and turned dials until he was happy with what he'd done.

'There.' Felix turned to Missy. 'I've programmed the plane to carry on flying until it reaches the coordinates I've entered.'

'The coordinates of the airbase?' Missy guessed.

Felix nodded. 'Now there's only one thing left for us to do.' He took a deep breath, picked up the on-board radio and spoke to Bill and Stella in the cockpit behind. 'On the count of three unlock the cockpit roof, stand up and jump over the edge. Then activate your parachute. I'll see you back on the ground below. Copy?'

Bill's voice came through the radio loud and clear. 'Copy.'

'One . . . two . . . three . . .'

The cockpit hatches clicked open. Felix and Missy climbed on to the wing with Bill and Stella just behind them.

'Trust me?' Felix smiled at Missy.

'Of course.' She smiled back.

The two friends leaped off the moving plane and hurtled through the air, the ground below speeding towards them.

17
Secrets and Promises

THUD!

SKID!

SLIDE!

STOP!

'I think I ripped a hole in the bottom of my flight suit!' Felix muttered as he stood up and inspected himself. 'My pants are hanging out!'

Missy frowned, getting to her feet and brushing herself down. 'Gross, Felix. The less said about your pants the better.'

'That was amazing!' Stella shouted. She and Bill had landed just a few metres away from Felix and Missy. 'Who knew jumping out of a plane could be so much fun!'

So that's where Missy gets her daredevil spirit from!

'We're only a couple of fields away from the airbase,' Bill said, unstrapping himself and Stella from the parachute. 'The plane must have . . .'

'Crashed into an airfield by now,' Felix confirmed.

'What will people think?' Stella said. 'When a plane with no pilot crashes into an airfield like that? A ghost plane.'

Felix and Missy exchanged a knowing look.

'I don't think it's something they'll forget in a hurry,' Missy said.

'They'll be talking about it for years to come,' Felix agreed, casting a look in Bill's direction.

'And Archie?' Stella wondered. 'Won't they wonder where he is? People are going to ask us what happened to him, what are we supposed to say?'

Bill shrugged. 'One thing's for certain, we can't tell them the truth.'

'No,' Felix said, trying to stuff his parachute back into his bag. There was way too much material, and half of it was hanging out and trailing along the ground. 'We need to protect Archie's new secret identity and the secrets of Churchill's submarine. As far as history's concerned, Archie has just disappeared.'

'When people ask us about him all we say is he was lost in battle,' Missy said. 'And if they ask for any more details then just explain that it's top-secret classified information.'

'Yeah, classified,' echoed Bill. 'We could tell them, but then we'd have to kill them.'

Stella smiled at Bill. 'Come on.' She stretched out

her hand towards him. 'Let's go back to base and face the colonel.'

Bill and Stella walked on ahead but Felix and Missy hung back so they could talk in private. Einstein crawled out of Felix's trouser pocket, his face a putrid shade of **green**.

'Einstein!' Felix smiled. 'Buddy, I'd almost forgotten about you. You've been so quiet this whole time.' Einstein's scales turned an even more disgusted shade of **green**. 'I know, I know, jumping out of a plane is probably not the way you'd want to spend an afternoon, but how else were we meant to get out of this?'

Einstein flashed a disgruntled shade of **purple** for 'yes' in reluctant agreement, before scuttling up Felix and hiding away in the breast pocket of his flight suit.

'Felix?' Missy said thoughtfully, as they walked through the field towards the airbase. 'Do you think that this was how history was always meant to play out? Do you think this was the only explanation for what happened to Archie, and why the plane crashed with no pilot?'

Felix nodded with certainty. 'Yes, I do. Otherwise everything we've done would have changed the course of history – and that's something we cannot do. Who knows what kind of trouble that would get us in?'

'So we were always meant to travel back in time and meet Bill and Stella, and we were always meant to crash-land the plane on the ocean, meet Churchill and leave Archie there?'

'Yes.' Felix nodded once again. 'And we were meant to parachute out of that plane so it flew and crash-landed with no pilot.'

Missy rubbed the patch of forehead between her eyes. 'Thinking about time travel gives me a headache sometimes.'

Felix shrugged. 'Of course it does, you're only human. Leave the complicated thinking to me.'

'There's one more thing that's bothering me,' Missy admitted.

'What's that?'

'Won't Bill recognize us in years to come? Then he'll know it was us who he met back in 1943 – he'll know we time travelled.'

'Leave it with me,' Felix said, starting to run ahead. 'Let me talk to him . . .'

Felix caught up with Bill and Stella. They were holding hands and talking in soft voices to one another.

'Sorry to break up the party,' Felix said, walking between them and forcing their hands apart. 'But I need a quick word with Bill, in private . . .'

Stella looked back towards Missy. 'Sure. I'll hang back and talk to Missy for a while.'

'Everything OK?' Bill asked, after Stella was out of earshot.

'There's something really important I need to say to you,' Felix said seriously.

'Are you going to tell me who you are?' Bill said, wide-eyed. 'How you know so much about everything and how you have all those crazy gadgets of yours?'

'No.' Felix shook his head. 'I can't tell you any of that stuff. I actually need you to make me a promise . . .'

Bill looked confused. 'Go on . . .'

'At some point in the future, two young children

212

are going to come to you and ask you about the war. Whenever that is – even if you have to wait seventy years – I want you to promise me that you'll tell them the story of the ghost plane, and of Archie's disappearance.'

'Seems a strange request,' Bill said, chuckling. 'But I guess I wasn't expecting anything straightforward, Felix. Sure.' He smiled down at him. 'I promise you that if two children ever come and ask me questions about the war, I'll tell them the story of the ghost plane.'

'Thank you.' Felix sighed, relieved. 'It's really, really important that you do.'

They all walked the rest of the way in silence. Each lost in their own thoughts . . .

Who is this kid and where did he come from? wondered Bill.

I wonder if every day with Bill will be as much of an adventure? thought Stella.

Never mind meeting Churchill and jumping out of a plane, thought Missy, *meeting Great-Grandma Stella has been the best thing about this adventure.*

This is the second time we've played a part in shaping history, realized Felix. **Time travel is so much more than just a game . . .**

Soon the gates to RAF Daws Hill were in sight. Two armed guards stood either side of the gates. They both reached for their radios as soon as they saw the bedraggled group of adventurers approaching.

This is it, Felix thought, breathing in deeply. **Let's hope Churchill's telegram arrived on time, otherwise we'll be lined up and shot for treason . . .**

18
A New Enemy

When they arrived back at the gates of RAF Daws Hill there was a small army of guards to greet them. They each had guns hanging visibly in their holsters, stern looks on their faces.

Great Galileo, don't tell me the telegram never made it . . .

At the front of the pack of guards was the colonel. With a face of stone, he looked each one of them up and down before pacing towards them and opening his arms.

'Heroes!' His face broke into a smile. 'You should have told me you were working with Churchill. I would have never had you locked up. I would have never had you shot at. I would never . . .

Where's Lieutenant Archie?'

Felix, Missy, Bill and Stella quickly exchanged glances.

'Colonel!' shouted a guard from the back of the pack, before any of them had a chance to explain what had happened to Archie. 'There are reports of a plane crash-landing on the other side of the airbase.'

The colonel spun around quickly. 'What?'

'They say it's one of ours, sir,' the guard added.

'Quickly,' shouted the colonel. 'Get as many men over to the field as you can. Rescue any survivors.'

There are no survivors, Felix thought. *No one was on the plane when it crashed . . .*

The colonel turned back towards Felix. 'Can you accept my apology for everything I had to do?'

'Yes,' said Felix. 'On one condition.'

'Anything,' the colonel replied quickly.

'You must never, ever mention that me or my friend –' he pointed at Missy – 'were here at RAF Daws Hill. You've never seen us before, never met us. You don't know anything about any secret missions or telegrams from Churchill. None of this ever happened. Understood?'

'Understood,' he replied. 'Now you'll have to excuse me, I must go – this plane, and whoever's on board – I need to help.'

Bill stood to attention and gave the colonel his best salute. 'Yes, sir!'

The colonel saluted back, before turning to one of the nearby guards and saying, 'Make sure they get back to base safely. Offer them food and water – they look exhausted.'

As the colonel and the other guards ran off to investigate the report of the crashed plane, only one guard remained.

That's the guard who looks exactly like Professor Aldini from our time!

'We'll go back to the boot room,' the guard said, waving for them to follow him. 'I'll radio the kitchens to make sure food and water is sent there for you.'

'And a change of clothes too?' Bill suggested, looking down at himself.

The guard growled in acknowledgement and walked on ahead.

'Can we stick around until the food comes out?' Missy whispered to Felix. 'I'm starving, and you're not going to get fed until you go back home and do all those chores for your mum.'

'Good point,' Felix said, feeling his tummy grumble. 'I'd totally forgotten that Mum was 'expecting me to build her a 3D TV this evening.'

'And 3D glasses,' Missy reminded him. 'And a bunch of other stuff.'

'We're definitely not leaving here on empty stomachs,' Felix agreed.

By the time they arrived back at the airbase boot room a selection of food had been laid out on a table for them, along with cups and jugs of water.

They thirstily gulped down their refreshing drinks as they surveyed the food on offer.

Corned beef, bread and butter, a few tomatoes, cold boiled potatoes and apples.

What was the obsession with gross tinned meat back in 1943?

'There is a war on, Felix,' Missy muttered to him, yet again seeming to know what he was thinking. 'Fresh meat is hard to come by.'

They all loaded their plates up with food. Stella and Bill stood at the table to eat, while Felix and Missy wandered away to sit down on a nearby bench. 'Aren't our normal clothes around here somewhere?' Missy whispered to Felix. 'We hid them somewhere in here before we changed into our flight suits and . . .'

'Are these what you're looking for?' the guard that looked just like Aldini snarled, standing in front of them and holding up two sets of clothes. 'They don't look like any items of clothing I've ever seen before. I can't think who else they would belong to around here. Nothing about you two seems to make sense . . .'

Felix snatched the clothes from him. 'These clothes are part of a classified top-secret operation and it is way above your clearance level to even be touching them!'

'What do you think I look like?' the guard sneered at them.

Professor Aldini! both Felix and Missy thought at the same time.

'An idiot?' the guard said. 'You might be able to fob the others off with your top-secret operation cover, but I know you.'

He knows us? What in the name of the galaxies does that mean?

'They're saying over the radio that there was no one on that plane that crashed. A ghost plane. Not possible. Every plane needs a pilot. And what happened to Archie, huh? Just disappeared into thin air? I know that you know the truth.' He stared Felix right in the eyes, daring him to tell him everything he knew. Felix stayed silent. 'You may have solved this mystery, but, trust me, next time I'll be right there with you – and I'll be the one to get there first.'

The guard gave Felix and Missy one final filthy look before storming out of the room, slamming the door behind him.

'What was all that about?' Missy said, looking as pale as Felix did. 'Everything he said . . . It's almost as if . . .'

'He knows the truth about us,' Felix finished. 'But that's impossible, Missy. We're the only ones with a time machine.'

Missy nodded. 'Speaking of time machines . . . do you think it's time?'

Felix nodded. 'Let's say goodbye.'

They both put down their half-eaten plates of food and walked over to Bill and Stella.

'Are you going?' Bill guessed.

Felix nodded. 'We can't stay.'

Stella lunged forward and threw her arms around Missy. 'Thank you for everything,' she said, squeezing Missy tightly. 'Thank you for introducing me and Bill, and for all your help on this adventure. We'll never forget you.'

'We'll never forget you,' Missy said to her great-grandmother, blinking away the tears in her eyes. 'Never.'

Felix shook Bill's hand. 'Remember what you promised?'

Bill nodded. 'I'll never forget.'

'I just need to ask you to do one more thing . . .' Felix said, taking his bag off his back and reaching about in it to find the time machine remote control.

'What's that?' asked Stella.

'Turn around, close your eyes and count to ten,' Missy said, still smiling from the long hug that Stella had given her.

Stella and Bill laughed as though Missy was joking, but when they realized she was serious they shrugged and did as she asked, turning around and closing their eyes. 'One . . . two . . . three . . .' they started to count.

'Ready?' Felix asked Missy, punching in the date and coordinates for home.

Missy nodded.

Felix peered into his top pocket. Einstein was still sulking, still a horrid shade of **green**. 'Sorry, buddy, we gotta go.'

With a final look in Bill and Stella's direction, Felix punched down his thumb on the green button on the remote control.

Felix and Missy felt the ground beneath their feet fall away from them. 1943 began to fade out of existence and soon they were hurtling through time and space . . .

19
A Sly Wink

> Gaga Bill and me are visiting mum @ the museum on saturday. wanna come?

Felix read over the text from Missy and replied straightaway.

> er, is the sun a dwarf star? of course I'll come!

> cool ☺ meet me @ gaga Bill's at 9 a.m. mum's driving.

Knock, knock, knock.

Gaga Bill opened the door to his little house and smiled at the sight of Felix on his doorstep. 'Felix!'

he said, waving him in. As Felix closed the door behind him Bill took him by the shoulders and stared straight into his eyes.

Felix stared back at the old man. He might look frail, his hair had thinned out and whitened over the years and his back hunched slightly with age, but looking into his eyes Felix saw the brave young fighter pilot he'd met back in 1943. *Only his body has changed,* Felix realized. *He's still the same person inside.*

Bill's pale milky eyes narrowed slightly and he gave him a small knowing nod. 'So nice to see you again, Felix. Although, you look different from the last time I saw you.'

He knows where we've been. He's not stupid. Let's just hope he doesn't ask how we got back there. The fewer people who know about the time machine the better!

'Really?' Felix bent down to pet Frosty, Bill's small dog.

Bill smiled. 'Yes. Older maybe – wiser perhaps.'

Felix looked up, unsure of what to say, but Bill had already walked off and was reaching for his coat.

'In here, Felix,' Missy shouted from Bill's living room.

Felix wandered into the living room to see Missy sitting on the sofa and holding the picture of Bill and Stella on their wedding day. She looked up and smiled sadly at Felix.

I know, he thought to himself. *I'm glad I met Stella too.*

'Time to go,' Bill shouted from the hallway. 'Your mum's car's outside, Missy.'

'OK, Gaga Bill,' Missy called back. 'Coming. Look —' Missy pointed to one of the many small pictures of planes framed on Bill's living-room walls. 'They look like . . .'

'Postcards.' Felix smiled. 'I remember thinking that when I was here before. Dozens of postcards of aeroplanes. And I bet if we took them out of their frames and opened them there would be nothing on the back.'

'You're right,' said Bill quietly, standing in the doorway and watching Felix and Missy. 'Every year on my birthday I had a postcard in the post. Never once was there a message on it, or a name of who sent it. But one thing I do know — whoever sent those cards lived a wonderful life. Each card was sent from a different corner of the globe. They stopped coming a few years ago.' Bill went quiet and stared at the cards.

Felix and Missy stood there in silence.

Felix could almost hear the blood pump around his body as he waited for Bill to speak again.

'I think you now know what happened to Archie, don't you?' Bill said, smiling as he looked across the dozens of postcards on his wall.

BEEP! BEEP!

'Your mother's waiting for us, Missy,' Bill said, turning and hobbling towards the front door. 'Better not keep her waiting,' he called over his shoulder.

'He knows!' Missy said in shock. 'He knows it was us back in 1943.'

'Maybe,' Felix agreed. 'But if there's anyone I trust to keep our secret then it's Bill.'

They bundled into the car and Missy's mother drove them to the museum. They listened to the radio, humming along to the tunes blasting out of the car speakers. 'Music these days,' Bill muttered, as Missy's mum pulled into the British Museum staff car park. 'It's nothing but noise. Nothing like the tunes we used to dance to in our day – now that was proper music.'

Felix and Missy smiled at each other, both

remembering the time they'd watched Bill and Stella dance the night away in 1943.

When they reached the entrance, Missy's mum punched in the security code to the museum's staff entrance and they followed her in.

A tall thin man with a permanent snarl etched on to his face was walking down the corridor towards them.

Professor Aldini!

'Professor Six,' Aldini said to Missy's mum. 'Bringing your family to work again I see. It's a wonder you ever get any work done . . .'

'It's my day off, Aldini,' Missy's mother replied with a tired sigh. 'I'm bringing my family to the museum to look around. There's no crime in that.'

'No,' he sneered. 'I suppose not.' He turned towards Felix and narrowed his eyes. 'You.' He outstretched his right hand and pointed straight at him.

A SCAR! He has a scar on his right hand!

'I've seen you lurking around the museum before; you're not Professor Six's family.'

'He's my daughter's best friend,' Missy's mum

said angrily. 'Now if you'll please excuse us.' She barged past Professor Aldini, Missy, Bill and Felix following behind.

Felix took one last look at Aldini's scar as he passed him. The hand reached out and grabbed the collar of Felix's coat. 'Stay away from this museum, boy,' Aldini threatened. His breath smelt like stale coffee and rotten cheese. 'And stay away from history – you know what I mean.'

Aldini dropped Felix and stormed off.

'Did you see that?' Missy whispered in Felix's ear, as Felix watched the door slam behind Aldini.

'The scar?' Felix nodded. 'Just like the guard back in 1943.'

'But you said it's impossible,' Missy pointed out. 'We're the only ones with a time machine.'

'There has to be some kind of rational explanation for it,' Felix said quietly.

There's a rational, mathematical explanation for everything in the universe. I just need to find out what this explanation is . . .

'And don't listen to a word he says,' Missy said, tugging Felix's coat so he turned around and looked at her. Professor Six and Bill had walked on ahead and he and Missy were alone in the corridor. 'You can't stay away from history, Felix. History needs you.'

'What do you mean?'

'If it wasn't for you and your time machine then there wouldn't even have been a ghost plane. Buckingham Palace would have been destroyed, and Archie would never have met Winston Churchill. Who knows what other mysteries you have the answer to? Was Prince Vlad the Impaler really a vampire? What really happened to the Lost City of Atlantis? And I really, really want to know the truth about Stonehenge . . . But first I think we should visit the Tower of London.'

'The Tower of London?'

'Don't tell me you're not just a little bit curious about all the mysterious things we could investigate there?' Her eyes lit up at the thought. 'The two young princes in the tower who disappeared from history? Missing crown jewels? The legend of Anne Boleyn's ghost? Apparently her headless ghost roams the stone halls and corridors in search of revenge. We should go back in time and investigate . . .'

'We have a school trip to the Tower of London coming up. We can investigate then,' Felix said quickly. 'I'm not making any promises about time travel, Missy, it's risky.'

She rolled her eyes at her friend. 'Come on.' Missy smiled. 'Gaga Bill's waiting for us –

I promised we'd show him around the Roman section before lunchtime.'

Felix watched Missy walk off towards Bill.

Maybe she's right, he thought to himself, standing alone in the dark corridor. *Do I have the key to unanswered mysteries in history? Do I need to time travel more? How do I know where I'm supposed to go and what I'm supposed to investigate?*

'Felix, come on!' Missy screamed back at him.

Felix smiled. *Black holes and comet tails, if I can't figure it out on my own then at least Missy will help me. She's the bossiest person I know!*

Acknowledgements

Thank you to my wonderful agent Victoria and to everyone at Quercus Children's Books for being awesome, inspirational, patient and supportive.

A huge thank you to my wonderful family for always being so supportive, for babysitting and for understanding that sometimes I need to disappear for a few hours with a laptop and an endless supply of coffee. And thank YOU for reading Felix Frost – maybe one day you'll build a time machine of your own!

Discover where the adventures began in ...

OUT NOW